He Knows I Know

Angel Bloxham

Copyright © 2023 Angel Bloxham

Starbrook Press—Madison, WI
ISBN: 978-1-3999-4866-1
eBook ISBN: 979-8-9861190-9-0
Library of Congress Control Number: 2023905645
Title: *He Knows I Know*
Author: Angel Bloxham
Digital distribution | 2023
Paperback | 2023

Dedication

For Hannah, for always believing in me

Chapter One
Faith

It was a flash of light that made my eyelids twitch open. Magnolia swirls settled into smooth walls. That's when I realised where I was. It took me a little longer to register that something gripped my wrist. I moved my eyes, feeling my neck was too weak to move my head. A slender arm caught my gaze. My eyes moved from the crinkled elbow to the plucked dry skin at the top of the arm, then past the shoulder. A woman. Her strawberry blonde hair brushed against the T-shirt that swamped her slim frame. Her finger tapped in sync with the beeps that rang across the room, but something caused her to stop. Anguished yet relieved, sobs spilled from her mouth.

"Nurse, she's awake! Faith has opened her eyes!"

Faith? A first glance didn't tell me who she was. Doctors raced in with inspecting hands, palpitating different parts of my body but my gaze never strayed away from the woman. In her bag, she found her mobile and pushed herself up from the creaky chair to dial a number. Her bag reflected different parts of the hospital room depending on how she tilted it. It felt like I was being given a tour of the space since I still couldn't move my neck to see it myself. The brightest reflection came from the monitor. Even curves moved in rows of horizontal lines. One row would leap every time the machine beeped, grabbing the woman's attention almost every time. I waited for her to further tilt her bag to catch sight of myself but as I turned my attention back to the woman, I realised the oversized T-shirt she wore was once a skin-tight dress.

"Eric, our baby's awake!"

I had no idea what I expected to discover as I gazed down. I knew it was metaphorical, but being a baby seemed to make more sense to me in some way. Instead, I saw a body clothed in a blue hospital gown with tubes pierced through areas of brown and purple skin. Strawberry blonde hair lay down on the stomach. The body that must belong to me.

"How are you feeling?"

It was the woman again. Her gentle hand reached out to touch mine. Only flakes of maroon nail polish remained on her oval-shaped nails. The nibbled skin surrounding the oval edge drew similar to the colour of her nail polish and at first glance, you would think she wasn't very good at painting her nails. I had to know who she was. My neck stiffened at my attempt to raise my head, so my eyes alone continued the journey and settled on her face. Her smooth neck contrasted with the creases beside her mouth and eyes. Her pouted lips drooped and her crow's feet trailed onto her forehead, leaving permanent lines even in her rested expression. Her once distinct cheekbones hid beneath a layer of loose skin and despite her sagging eyelids, her green eyes were large.

Then a tall man barged into the room, interrupting my attempt to answer the question I knew I had no answer to.

"It's okay darling, we're here."

The man's face looked smoother than the woman's did. His brown, bushy eyebrows made his small, circle eyes look sunken. His curly hair had receded, but I couldn't figure out his age. He then leapt to hug me and a sharp pain crippled my chest. He quickly shifted his focus to the woman.

"When did they say she could come home?"

It was then when I attempted to speak, but the casing over my mouth muffled my words. They did, however, understand what I meant. The smiles on both the woman's and the man's faces faded. The doctor looked up from his piled paperwork and a calm voice followed.

"Memory loss is typical in patients who have experienced the intensity of Faith's coma. But it doesn't mean her memory will not return."

Disbelief deepened in the doctor's voice when he peered down to confirm my results.

"Her body functions as if nothing happened. But we will keep her in to monitor her in case anything changes."

They were my parents, the man and the woman. That's who they claimed to be at least. Mum stayed as long as the visiting hours allowed. I'd notice the fresh flowers in the vase beside me spring up out of nowhere every few days. She'd comb my hair every day whether I wanted it to happen or not. As soon as she sat down in the chair, she'd take out her purple-tinted comb.

"This is the same comb my mother used to brush my hair with as a child," she said, as she'd begin at the ends, combing up to my roots.

Knowing exactly what to expect from Mum's visits became comforting. She planned what she would do with every minute she stayed with me. Granted, most of it included stories from my past, and her face would fill with disappointment as I drew a blank.

Dad didn't stay as long as Mum or visit as often. And as a result, his visits were less predictable. He only came on his own once without Mum by his side. For the first time, the tense atmosphere dissipated and I wished there had been more time when it was just the two of us. Mum wasn't with him that day, but she was in the hospital. She was demanding any nurse's help to get more information about my memory loss. Because of the heaviness in her brows when she entered the room to join Dad and me, I knew the doctors had relayed the same message they had told us. It was the one thing Mum found the hardest to get past.

I watched the days and weeks pass from the turned pages of the small calendar sitting near the fresh flowers. Each day had a quote that read identically to the previous but varied wording. Mum switched the page to the correct date, so I assumed it must have been something she had brought. The optimistic and uplifting quotes seemed more for her than for me.

'*When it rains, look for rainbows,*'

were the days' words looking back at me. The 11th. The day the doctors finally approved me to go home.

It was yet another thing that Mum had planned, making me prepared and out of the hospital much faster than it seemed even she had anticipated. The bright hospital room made the outside world appear dim. I knew they were being overly cautious as they transported me out of the hospital in a wheelchair. I imagined if I'd been walking, finally breathing fresh air rather than my recycled carbon dioxide, it would have given me a spring in my step. But, it didn't matter how I got to the car; all that mattered was that I got there and was out of that hospital room.

Dad wheeled me to an all-black, well-kept Mercedes-Benz. He pressed a button on a keypad to open the car's doors. He fixed his eyes on my face as if he was waiting for my reaction to his seemingly new device. I let out a surprised gasp. It appeared that pleasing Dad was simpler than pleasing Mum.

I pushed to climb in myself but, despite my protests, Dad carried me out of the wheelchair and buckled me into the back seat. I observed the wheelchair sitting outside the car as he closed my door and stepped into the driver's seat. I figured the chair was only with me out of Mum's request. Then we began our journey home, wherever home was.

The car slowed in front of the drive gate, which opened as it neared. It made me wonder if the gate was also controlled by the same keypad that unlocked the car doors.

The crackling noises under the car's wheels stamped concern over Mum's face as we pulled into the driveway. I watched as she got out and picked up the stray stones scattered across the road. My gaze followed as she moved from one side of the gate to the other. I noticed a 'sold' sign nestled among bushes and immediately swung my head to face the house, realising I had yet to glance at the place that beckoned to be my home.

Dark symmetrical windows sat on the smooth white front, and a manicured lawn with high hedges surrounded the whole property. Dad opened the car door beside me and with Mum still distracted by the stones, I jumped out and walked towards the porch doors.

I had no expectations of home life with them, let alone living in a house that big. As I envisioned what might be inside, my zero expectations began to grow. But inside, the house stood bare.

Dad motioned for me to walk through the open door with his hand. I felt I was about to step through an unseen seal, one that had been waiting inside for me for months. One that had only seen my previous self come in. I was about to discover who I was from the same, but different eyes. Would taking the initial step bring memories flooding back to me? I paused for a moment before moving my feet. I had to take my time since it was impossible to know how my body would react. That was until I heard the clipping of Mum's heels pick up to a sprint.

Before I could react, she took my hand and pulled me through the open front door, past a gleaming white, marbled open plan kitchen and into what appeared to be a once-lived-in lounge. The glare from the French doors sparkled off the polished dark oak floorboards.

There were five boxes sitting in the far-right corner with a three-piece suite. Dad, after catching up to us, straightened the brown leather sofa and the one similar chair. Mum let go of my hand and paced over to behind the pile of cardboard boxes. Her shoes echoed across the room, and I watched each urgent step she took. Finally, she picked up a large wooden box from behind the stack and walked back over to place it down in front of me. Dad let out a long sigh the moment it caught his attention.

"Jan, please, not now. She's only just got home."

"What is it?" I questioned.

Unconcerned about what Dad had said, she revealed a heap of crumpled paperwork and handed me a small pile. 'Faith Mathews' were the only words that seemed recognisable to me in the sea of certificates.

"You missed your 16th birthday while you were in the hospital," Dad said as he took my birth certificate from my hands.

I was 16? Not once had it occurred to me to even ask my age. The only time my age entered my thoughts was when I anticipated seeing baby limbs as I looked down at my body in the hospital bed. At the very least, it didn't feel strange for it to be my age. I looked up at Dad to ask more about this unopened topic, but tears filled his eyes, and I was at a loss for words. Still having no memory of anything before the coma started to make me feel sociopathic. Seeing Dad like that brought me no emotion but confusion. How was I supposed to empathise with something I don't remember living? How was I meant to comfort grieving parents when I was the grief? Once my mind fell blank with any words I could say to comfort him, I looked back into the box.

A worn, white piece of paper in one corner had the words 'Entry of marriage' printed on it. I pulled it from the heap, thinking it must belong to Mum and Dad. Names in tiny joined-up writing read as 'Janice White' and 'Eric Mathews.'

"White, my maiden name," Mum clarified. Her light smile fell to a picture of gloom. "Poor father."

Dad sat beside Mum on the sofa, putting his arm around her to console her. Once the tears dried from her eyes, Mum handed me a glossy photo that she said was of me. I'd seen my face in Mum's compact mirror and again in the reflections of cars in the hospital carpark, but never in detail. I looked exactly like Mum. For a moment, all I could see were my enormous green eyes. My head faced forward but I figured if I rotated it to the side, the camera would have captured the identical bump on Mum's nose. My gaze followed my tightly braided hair down to an embroidered school logo.

"We're moving you to a new school," Mum expressed.

I turned to the five boxes I remembered seeing as I walked in.

"Are you sending me away?"

Mum chuckled. It was the first time I saw her do so. "No, darling, we're moving house."

The air then became quiet. Mum appeared to be in a daze, leaving Dad and me to continue the conversation by ourselves. There was so much I needed to say, so much I wanted to say. For weeks, I'd been mulling questions over, but there wasn't a moment where it felt right to ask. Mum set out her visits to me, and it felt easier to stick with them without causing any interruptions. I thought I missed an opportunity when Dad came to see me alone, but the peace his visits brought was so pleasant that I was afraid to spoil it.

The silence had become awkward, and Dad began to pat his knees.

"Right, let me show you your room." He exhaled the words like an atmosphere break.

My bedroom was the first door we came to upstairs. As I pushed down the handle, a flood of bubble gum pink welcomed me. Then, out of the corner of my eye, I saw Dad leave to return down the stairs. I hoped he wouldn't bring the box with my documents back to me. Every new piece of knowledge I had to take in and accept had begun to overload my thoughts.

Only a single strand of Polaroid photographs, braided in fairy lights, remained on the plain rear wall. I was curious about what led them to leave specific photos up as they took the others down. Each shot radiated happiness. Girls dressed in mini dresses and red lipstick with arms clung to whoever was next to them. Balloons and party poppers in the hands of guys seeking to scare everyone else with the loud noises. I saw myself, at least that's who I assumed the strawberry blonde hair belonged to. I was standing away from the camera, kissing a guy. His face was also hidden from view. A romantic moment caught with a click. A click now wiped from my memory.

Dad reappeared, interfering with my thoughts. He sat on the mattress in the centre of the floor, clutching a panda-shaped mug. His words fell mute as they left his mouth. Questions began to build higher in my mind, each threatening to spill out of my tongue. He raised his voice and continued speaking when he noticed I wasn't paying attention.

"...My business is why I have no time, though. It's 24/7. Sometimes I envy those who can leave their jobs at 5 p.m and forget about it until 9 a.m the next day."

A part of what he spoke sank into my head. While in the hospital, I wondered why he didn't come as often as Mum. His business was most likely how they afforded to live in such a lavish home.

I realised I was about to lose another opportunity to ask the most crucial question bubbling inside my brain.

"What put me in a coma?"

Interrupting Dad seemed to have startled him. He placed the mug next to the mattress and adjusted his posture to face me.

"We were expecting you to tell us. Nothing on your body, inside or out, suggested any injury, which confused every doctor we met. We had the best doctors in the country running every test. They labelled it a medical mystery." I could see him fighting back the tears as he spoke, "we feared we were going to lose you."

He inhaled and wiped his tears after a second of collecting himself. Our eyes fixed together, and a sad, closed-mouth smile indented his smile lines.

"If there's anything you need, just shout," he said, sincerely.

I returned his half-smile and watched him leave my room, closing the door behind him. I felt the weight of Dad's words growing heavier as I laid on the prepared sheets on the mattress. I was forced to picture myself in a hospital once more. Wires inserted into my skin as I remained motionless. The life I lived before leaking away from my memories. Mum's deteriorating hope eating away at her flesh. Her need for me to wake up, her need for me to live. The need so strong she'd forfeit her own life. Her need for answers, for cures. I imagined her sobs absorbing into Dad's shoulder as he soothed her. His calm demeanour belied a broken heart. My eyes then opened, but my past remained closed. The anti-climax. I failed them.

I didn't need anything from Dad. It seemed he couldn't help me with anything anyway. He and Mum spent the next few days packing the remaining items into boxes and loading them onto removal vans parked in our driveway. I hadn't anticipated having to move so quickly. I still wasn't sure if it was a coincidence that I was out of the coma in time for the move, or if we would have moved at all if I was still in the hospital. It felt good to have their focus turned to something else though. For the first time, I didn't feel the need to be the person they knew before.

**

"What's the name of my new school?" I asked as I watched a sign pass by the car reading, '*Welcome to Dawnton Town.*'

"Dawnton High." Dad glanced at me in the rear-view mirror. "You'll be fine, sweetheart." His comforting smile reflected back at me.

It was the night we moved into our new house. The night before they expected me to start my first day at the new school. Everything was moving too quickly. I considered inventing aches and pains since I was confident that Mum and Dad would believe me. It would guarantee that I missed school, but I wasn't sure if it would also ensure a return to that soul-sucking hospital room. So, I opted to remain silent after considering the options. The name of the school was at least known to me now, I reasoned. That built upon the other two things I already knew about it. The first I discovered through overheard discussions between Mum and Dad about my education and potential debt problems. It was obvious that they were paying a lot of money for me to attend, though how much I wasn't quite sure. The second was less about the school and more about the time I would be spending there.

"At first, one lesson per day; the rest of your lessons will be home tutored by yours truly," Dad informed me.

I agreed silently, which was becoming more natural as the days passed.

I assured myself that the anxiety I was feeling was normal. Starting a new school is terrifying for anyone, whether or not they have awoken from a coma. It was for the best, I thought. If they didn't know who you were before, there would be fewer issues. It could be a much-needed fresh start for us all.

After passing through several trees, a stretch of untamed grassland appeared around a silhouette of a two-story house. Mum's whimpering, which I'd heard since we passed the sign announcing our arrival into Dawnton town, worried me. She was the first to slowly waddle in, Dad and I quickly followed. The front door opened into a kitchen. Countertops piled high with clutter matched the height of the unwashed dishes left in the sink. Two plates sat side by side on the wooden dining table: one was spotless, while the other had dried gravy smudged around the edge. I began to doubt that we were at the correct address. That's when I noticed the brushing of Mum's feet had come to a stop. I watched in the dim light of the coal fireplace as she raised her tired head to peer straight across the room. Her limp body fell to the floor.

Chapter Two
Melissa

Dawnton High had begun to rot. New students stopped arriving, many current students never returned, and our town's houses began to fall into disrepair. Dawnton town was once an insignificant name written on a map until the day that marked its history forever. The disruption of the town left the school almost teacher-less for the first month, creating a swarm of animals and leaving them to roam free. Fewer hours and increased pay brought most of them back, but they never seemed stable enough to have returned.

Since the incident, every teacher doubled as a class therapist, never raising their voice. They would hint at an announcement over the course of a week if they thought it would disrupt the routine at school. Although, we always managed to handle the news better than the teachers. Mr Adams had spent the previous week preparing us for the information he was about to give.

"Listen up, everyone. A new student will be joining you in English next period, so I don't want you to panic as w—"

Bea flicked her golden locks into the eyes of Gabriella Lucas. I forced a laugh because it was my responsibility. Having friends was always so distant from reality until something unimaginable happened in the schoolyard last term. It began with a sound I used to dread.

"Melissa? Mel?"

Overwhelming panic gripped my chest as I recognized the voice calling my name. Bea and Victoria caught me attempting to escape them both the day before, so I knew running away wouldn't be so easy this time.

"I asked my father if he could drive you home. Only if you want that of course," Victoria offered.

I stood there waiting for a chanting circle to form around her. This had happened too often for me to fall into the same trap again. Instead, as her tanned legs began to move, her beautiful hair bounced in the wind. I had never seen her smile that warmly before.

Gabriella Lucas was standing in the corner of the schoolyard. As we exchanged glances, her stance shifted. Gabriella separated herself from everyone when her naked photo circulated at school. Someone blurred the girl's face, and the hair colour differed from Gabriella's, yet everyone continued to believe it. Victoria and Bea had been best friends with her before it happened. Gabriella was well aware of her power and exploited it to gain control over others. I saw it as punishment for her being so cruel. Accepting the look printed was jealousy rather than concern, I followed Victoria like a lost duckling.

A sprinkle of respect travelled across the school because I, Mel, was friends with the most popular girls at Dawnton High.

As the start of English drew near, descriptions of the new student were being passed around. Bea wrapped her hair around her pen as she glanced at the classroom door. "I'm curious to see if he'll have a strong jaw-line."

Rolling his eyes, Sam responded, "it's impossible to know if they're gonna be a boy, Bea."

Sam hadn't been at Dawnton High long. He was the only person I knew who received a scholarship to attend Dawnton, aside from myself. Sam and I were confident more students also received scholarships, but a peculiar etiquette of that class of wealth was that they frowned upon you if you discussed how much your family had. Hence, no one knew the extent of anyone's estate. Though, it didn't stop some from dropping how much their dad spent on their new designer bag.

When Sam and I first met, we instantly became friends. He was different from others in my year. It was his accent that first caught my attention. The phrases he used and the way he dropped the t's in his words comforted me. Perhaps it was because it was how I used to speak until the school forced it out of me. He was confident in what he said, telling you how he felt to your face. That, within itself, was a rarity in Dawnton Town.

On his first day, he said to me, "you know, I never thought I'd end up in a place like this. In a private school? I'll never be able to wrap my 'ead around it."

I replied that I felt the same on my first day at Dawnton. At that point, we learned we both had scholarships, which marked the beginning of our friendship. I didn't know anyone who disliked him, at least not how they disliked me.

By this time, I usually would have added to the conversation. But I hadn't spoken to Sam since I became friends with Victoria and Bea, so I watched from afar.

Bea's throat swallowed her gum. She would make it clear for the person who angered her to see. Like a wild animal's warning once they sense danger. And she was ready to strike.

"It's possible that they'll be like you, Sam. Didn't they only transfer you here because of the heroin needle they found in your bag?"

An evil smirk followed. Immediately, I turned my head hoping they wouldn't notice my lack of laughter. Sam only trusted one person to keep his secret. Only I knew about his time in rehab before moving to Dawnton High. I wanted him to roar. A punch wouldn't have been as devastating as seeing the brokenness behind his eyes. The thrill of sharing an unspoken secret with Victoria and Bea had potentially ruined Sam's life at Dawnton forever.

I scanned the faces of the class and, to my surprise, no one heard what Bea had revealed. Panic soon followed relief. Empty promises had become unfamiliar. Was this the beginning of the humiliation?

"Saved by the bell," Victoria chuckled.

Head down and walk forward, were the five words I repeated during the lesson change. The brief stroll to the next lesson seemed to last an eternity. I needed to get to English before Sam arrived; I couldn't bear facing him.

I had spent the beginning minutes of the lesson staring at the classroom door, expecting Sam to walk in at any moment. I noticed a shadow appear on the corridor wall, and it was moving closer. I turned my head and held my breath, uncertain what to say or do as he come close. But then silence overtook the class. A stream of light glistened through a figure's contours as long hair swayed in unison with their hesitant steps. Strands of Strawberry blonde hair emerged from the light, distinguishing an outline to a face. A gentle flow of peace travelled through my veins. Of course, everybody's shifted attention prompted the feeling, but I couldn't help but wonder why it was so intense.

"You must be Faith Matthews. Welcome to Dawnton High!" I could see Mrs Beckett quieting the peculiar squeals she lets out when she's excited.

The girl smiled nervously. She was the first student to arrive at Dawnton High in months, and Mrs Beckett struggled to keep her composure.

"Well, seeing you're standing, why don't you tell us a bit about yourself?"

I wanted to break the engagement of everybody from Faith. Her uneasiness was making me uncomfortable.

"I just moved to this town."

Mrs Beckett could no longer ignore the continuous stream of emails on the classroom projector. As soon as she sat at her desk, Faith began to stutter.

"B-but I don't know anything else."

The classroom was filled with giggles. What did Faith have to hide? When past students didn't return, people stopped caring about new students. I often wished I hadn't begun school in the first years since it's easier to be yourself when no one knows who you were before. But I knew her grasp wouldn't stay as strong, and whatever's hidden would soon be common knowledge. Although, I would not be the one to tell anyone.

Distress paused Mrs Beckett's face as she sat in the same awkward position. She straightened her short legs and faced Faith as she became aware of the gazes on her.

"I'm so sorry, Faith. I didn't read the email when I should have."

The same anxious smile left Faith's mouth.

Mrs Beckett continued, "I'm sorry for your loss."

Faith appeared confused when Mrs Beckett gave her condolence. But unfortunately, it wouldn't be the first time she had misread an email.

"Everyone's already in groups, so you have full choice of which one you would like to join," Mrs Beckett added.

Instantly, Faith's ocean green eyes travelled in my direction.

Faith joined our group without hesitation, much to Victoria and Bea's displeasure. But for the first time since Victoria approached me, I couldn't verbally agree with them.

I would always be absent on the group project days, as it's difficult to form a group when no one wants to work with you. It was different this term. But when Victoria revealed her in-depth plan for the project, I wondered if working alone would have been more beneficial to me.

"What are you guys working on?"

Suspecting Victoria and Bea would completely ignore any words that left Faith, I began to answer.

"A persuasive writing project, persuading that you have solved the unsolvable."

I watched her face drop as Victoria revealed her topic idea.

"We all came to the same decision: 'Why can we still smudge quick-drying nail polish after it has cured for the indicated amount of time? So, we're not changing it."

When Faith agreed rather than involving her opinion, I sighed in relief.

As expected, the piercing sound of the fire alarm appeared, and the routine followed. Because of the decline in new students joining the school, what used to happen once every few times a new student arrived at Dawnton, now happens every new arrival. After acting surprised, Mrs Beckett pushed Faith towards me and rushed us to the schoolyard. Choosing me to be in charge of a clueless newbie. But it wasn't all that horrible. Her gentle manner took away my thoughts from all that was happening with Sam.

While standing at the back of the fire escape line, a soft, saliva-filled lick touched my calf. Before my body could process what happened, a delighted call left Faith's mouth.

"Milo! Hello boy!"

I moved my eyes to the fence behind me. Milo was a three-legged dark chocolate Labrador, unlike any other in our town. Milo was *my* dog.

"Didn't you say you'd only recently moved here?" I responded as fast as my brain could grasp the confusion.

Faith's astonished look left me undecided if it was genuine. I needed answers to my questions about everything that happened that day, but Milo was my priority. I squeezed my way through the cloudy metal fence, confident that the class headcount had finished, and began following the cobbled path into the trees.

The trip to the house had a triumphal feel to it. Milo had a habit of escaping when Louise left him alone for more than an hour, but I figured his three legs would at least keep him at bay until the school day had ended.

School used to be one of the few places where I could escape home. Guilt kept me from ever complaining to anyone about my childhood. Although I essentially had no Mum or Dad, Aunt Louise had always been there to pick up the pieces. Her sweet expression remained the same no matter how many times I created a scene. She'd take off her square-framed glasses to show her warm copper eyes. Our brownish-hued hair was the only physical similarity we shared. My entire life, people would tell me my features resembled my mother's. Those words alone used to make me cry as a child. Her wicked dark eyes staring into mine as her thin lips spewed beads of venom. Her rounded nose and flaring pointed nostrils, as I struggled to recall what had re-awakened her rage. Even yet, it was something I despised hearing.

It felt strange being home alone. The absence of the twins, Macy and Maddie, screaming with laughter while Louise performs her fictional stories, had the house feeling lonely. Macy and Maddie were Louise's children, my cousins. She discovered the twin's pregnancy the same day her husband received a terminal bone cancer diagnosis. Louise doesn't speak much of him to me anymore, but I wished she would.

Since Louise bought the house, our kitchen had remained in the same 1980s style. I was almost offended when she told me it had grown on her. It had to be the comfort I got from the overpowered heater because I could feel it growing on me too. Taped to the counter's edge was a piece of paper. *'I'm not sure when I'll be back, money is in the Empty jam jar; treat yourself to a takeaway. Love Louise.'*

The day would determine how many years in prison Michael would spend. Louise had earlier notified the school that I would be absent. But, after understanding that I wasn't going to sit at home and wait to find out how long my brother would be imprisoned, she headed for court. She continued to refuse to tell me why he was in trouble. Michael had never sought to be a part of my life, not in the way a brother should. Perhaps Louise assumed I didn't care.

Milo's sudden bark seemed louder with nobody home. With no sound from the doorbell, I assumed the post had arrived. A single unsealed envelope was sitting on the recently chewed doormat. I noticed my name in black ink when I turned the envelope over. I took the thickly worded letter out cautiously.

'You carnt tell anyone you have resived this letter...'

Chapter Three
Faith

But it was so distinct, so vivid that I couldn't ignore it. A dog looking precisely as Milo did, with that name tied to him. It appeared out of nowhere in my mind, like a memory would. As I watched Melissa disappear into the trees, it became clear I had made a mistake. How could it have been a memory when she didn't even know who I was? I shouldn't have said anything. I decided then, in case others would react the same way, to keep my presumed memory to myself.

The pull I felt towards Melissa began to disrupt my thoughts about Milo. My anxiety seemed to float into a cloud of comfort when I saw her.

I looked around the schoolyard for something to distract me from my thoughts. Students stood in long lines, waiting for teachers to call their names. The lines were rippling with nudges and hugs as laughter and yelling echoed around me. I remained motionless, stunned. I turned around to face the trees, half expecting to see Melissa coming back through them. But she hadn't returned. I decided to refocus my attention back on the schoolyard. Victoria and Bea were the only two people I recognised. Still, they didn't seem inviting when I asked them about their project idea. The fears I had about starting a new school were becoming a reality. I worried I ruined the chance I had to finally feel normal.

***

The hour-long lesson at school felt less than the hour-long lessons at home as the days passed. People told me how fortunate I was not to have to work the entire day at school. School was a source of dread for everyone. Everyone but me, it seemed. Due to my doctor's request, I had to do most of my schoolwork at home so my parents could keep a close eye on me. I could see why it was necessary, but I wish it wasn't so. I was grateful to Dad for taking the time to teach my classes, given how many hours he worked, but going to school felt like an escape from the stress that persisted at home. Mum or Dad hadn't spoken about the night we moved in.

Every morning, Mum waited, eyes glued to the clock, until the moment it changed. 9 a.m. I watched her take a tube of pills and swallow them one by one. She sat in her wooden chair in front of her bedroom window, repeating it daily. Dad would only ever acknowledge it by their code word.

"Love, did you want me to pick up the pinks? I'm popping into the pharmacy."

I understood it every time.

A new relative would daily regurgitate the same stories of my younger self. I began to know them word for word, even convincing myself that a breakthrough had happened. Which, of course, it hadn't. Frustration began to overlap my hopefulness. With my mind only taking me back to the memory with Milo, I knew I had to try and approach it.

"Did we ever own a dog, Mum?"

"Darling, no way. From afar, they're okay, but I'd never let them into my house."

The daily phone calls became a desperate attempt to get a yes as I described a memory with a three-legged Labrador. At my last effort, I felt hopeless. Anxiety began to tiptoe into my thoughts, and I felt I had to convince myself it was merely a passing observation.

I saw Melissa in English the next day, but she didn't seem present. Something captivated her mind, and she spent the entire lesson dazed. I wondered if I should have said something, told her I overheard somebody talking about a three-legged chocolate lab named Milo, and that was how I knew it. But I wasn't prepared for any follow-up questions, and if I lied, I wouldn't know where to begin. Worse, I'd have no idea where to stop. The alternative was to tell the truth, but even *I* had no idea what that meant.

In the end, that lesson was pretty meaningless. The group project didn't progress any further than the previous lesson. Victoria and Bea were in charge of the group discussions and never stayed on topic. The talks they would have with each other were fascinating to listen to. But the more I heard, the more I realised that I would not have joined a group with those two if I had had another chance. Melissa remained quiet while they chatted. I assumed it was because she was wary of me, but as the lesson went on, it was only me that she had spoken to.

I watched the three of them and wondered if their friend group dynamics had always been this way. It was clear they were looking for Victoria's approval. Bea would leave every sentence open-ended so she could amend it if Victoria disagreed. I'm not sure how Victoria got that power, but I could see she knew how to wield it.

Still, it felt easier being at school than at home.

I had forgotten the need to return to the hospital until I heard Mum's calls from downstairs, jolting me out of sleep.

"Faith, it's time to wake up, I thought I set your alarm 15 minutes ago," and, "we can't be late for your appointment, not today!"

For a week, Dad only spoke with us when transporting the phone to me. It became clear that he practically lived in his office. He was adamant that his duty was to protect us from any stress, so only he should be the provider in the home. I knew Mum's fear of her and Dad's relationship fading. He gave her the strength to leave their bed every morning. Even with Dad's constant reassurance, I still heard her question it.

Muffled voices left their bedroom.

"Just leave your work for one day!"

"I have so much to do, Jan. Let me know how she gets on. I'm sure everything's going to be fine."

Mum set a plan for us to travel to the hospital as a family, so it was difficult for her to accept that it was now the two of us.

The change between the two towns was surprising and originally went unnoticed. As we drove closer, the unresponsive streets of melancholy transitioned to an ease of calmness. Mum's company was becoming more enjoyable than it had been before. I couldn't

ignore the feeling of unconditional love she had for me.
I tried so hard but couldn't feel the same towards her.

After a few hours on the road, the route became
familiar. Finally, a real memory was resurfacing; it was
the moment I had been waiting for.

Our old house.

Amid my disappointment, I noticed Mum leave the
car.

"I cannot believe it!"

Her stern expression intrigued me enough to leave
the car myself. Mum gestured to the floor as she
noticed me approaching. Our driveway, which was
previously stone filled, had been redone with concrete.
I wasn't sure why she felt disappointed since Mum and
Dad hadn't been the house owners for a while.

"It would enrage your father so much if he were
here. The amount we used was so costly."

I nodded and followed Mum back into the car,
realising how little I knew about Dad. Mum would tell
me everything about her life, teaching me the outline
of her past until I could recite it word for word. But I
never once heard Dad speak about his.

"Does Dad have any siblings?"

"Your father?" Mum asked, her tense eyebrows
relaxing, "he was an orphan. His blood relatives are
unknown to him."

She told me of his childhood in the orphanage. Dad
was forced to work on farmland without rest from the
age of nine, while the leaders beat him and force him
to remain silent. His physical and emotional scars
remained fresh, and Mum said that is why he prefers to
not bring up painful memories by dwelling on the past.

As she spoke, I wondered if she should have first asked Dad if it was okay to tell me.

Then came a smile.

"Your Grandfather said I was foolish to get married so young."

She stared ahead through tears, and her smile straightened.

"Poor father."

Mum hadn't elaborated on Granddad's death. It was only when Mrs Beckett urged me to talk to Mum about him, I realised a granddad once existed. Dad restricted the subject, and Mrs Beckett knew an uncomfortable amount. It felt as if there was something more that they were not telling me.

Parked in the same space as before, we arrived at the hospital. The ticks on the clock were becoming weighted, with each second feeling longer than the previous. We sat in silence, waiting for my results. This time the doctors inspecting hands felt intrusive, and I felt relieved when it had finished. I hoped it would be the last time we would need to go there. I glanced over to Mum, wondering if she felt the same. I often tried to figure out what thoughts captured Mum. When in conversation her mind drifts, her eyes barely sticking to their pupils. But if I join, she stays in reality. Almost as if she feels she has to.

"Mrs Mathews, good news!"

The doctor drew our focus back into the room.

"Weekly checks are no longer needed. But, if you experience anything out of the ordinary, it is important to tell me immediately."

Mum and I exchanged a relieved sigh as we nodded in unison.

The chaotic crowd of worn-down, medical blue chairs in the waiting area were now parallel to each other. At the end, a pair of eyes widened. Then a blur of a figure bolted towards me.

"Faith! Finally! How are you? I got the message saying you are back for the day. I've missed you so much."

As my eyes adjusted, a confident, slender guy appeared in front of me. The beams from the hospital lights obscured his face. Mum continued calling him 'E', so I waited for another name to try to piece something together.

They told my story the same way. Mum wrote a detailed diary from when I was in a coma until the day I awoke. Both memorised everything word for word, ensuring descriptions were not misheard.

"Faith, this is Ethan."

She paused, waiting for my reaction.

"He was your boyfriend."

His smooth brown hair matched an image that flashed in my mind. The kissing Polaroid. I attempted to compose a sentence to respond, but his head was already lowered in sadness.

"How about taking her to the Almond Café? You two used to be there all the time!"

Ethan's features were re-energised.

"Would you join me, Faith? It could be the beginning of some answers?"

"Okay."

It wasn't as if I could say no and let him be on his way, waving and shouting 'nice to have met you anyway' as he left. Even though it was what I so desperately wanted to do.

It wasn't a particularly long walk, but it was enjoyable. I hadn't eaten lunch yet and I wondered if Ethan hadn't as well. But I sensed that he was only hungry for what we once had.

The café was a small and confined building, separate from the nearby shops. It had no sign to show it was a café, but an almond sticker stuck on the front window.

We walked in, him first and me trailing behind like a lost duckling. I displayed a false hope as Ethan pointed to the single rose-patterned booth in the far corner.

He caught a server's attention as we sat down. I thought the booth had an unusual smell, close to an elderly person's home. Was that a memory? Mum or Dad had never brought me to one. Whatever it was, I was sure that the soft material chairs couldn't be particularly sanitary. A waitress set down two-pint glasses of lemonade in front of us.

"You pretended lemonade was your favourite when we first met, and I thought..." Ethan's voice faded into the sounds of nearby tables.

I was sure there was no other way to interpret Mum's explanation. He's unknown to me, a stranger. How could a relationship survive such a loss?

Ethan's voice peaked again, "and Jess said she's so jealous of what we have and how much she admires our love."

"Look, Ethan. You seem like such a nice guy, but I don't think we can continue as we were."

He took a breath and looked me in the eyes, "I know, I just hoped."

His body began to deflate, and I watched a single tear drown in his lemonade. It wasn't my intention to cause pain, but pretending to love in an undiscovered life would only ever halt me.

I hadn't understood my own emotions until that point. Was the old Faith a liar? How did she manage to be so convincing? The issue wasn't the process of trying to rekindle my love for Ethan; it was with who he was. What he was. A guy. When I loved girls.

Chapter Four
Melissa

It was for five years.

His sentence was for five minuscule years of his existence. He'd never appear in my thoughts again, forgotten from my life just like the rest of them. Like Mum. Both in prison, internally rotting. It was where they belonged.

Louise walked through the door, wiping away a fallen tear from the raw skin under her eyes. Mum and Michael never carried such emotions, such empathy. The only monster I feared as a child was the potential that mine would awaken, and I would become who they were. Louise placed her hand on my wrist and barely spoke my brother's sentence. But, unbeknownst to her, I already knew. Michael almost killed Milo in the dogfights, leaving him with only three legs. Why you couldn't leave Milo alone for more than five minutes was finally clear. But, I had to keep the letter a secret, or I'd lose my dad too. The last paragraph kept replaying over in my head.

'I love you so vry so much. Wich is why I need to meet you to reveal somethin to you. Meet me at Morie park 7 p.m tommoroe. Please dont tell anyone your coming, please trust me.'

The mistakes were too obvious to blame my brain for over-correcting the words. How could I place my trust in something when he was unable to spell the word, please, yet is pleading? But I was aware I was being too harsh.

I knew I had to see him. At school, I stopped agreeing with Victoria and Bea's every word and began avoiding them. It was the only way to get through how much they wounded Sam. He wasn't in school again, and neither was Faith. She would change the reason for her entire family's trip back to her old town. But I knew she had yet to tell the truth. So with no one around, I devised a strategy for meeting Dad.

I knew Louise would be picking up the twins from school in the minutes after I got home, so I had to move quickly. It wouldn't even take a half hour to walk to Morie park. But aware it was my only chance; I grabbed my school bag and pushed the front door handle down. A family picture captured my eyes as I was about to run. The only family picture with any importance to me. Louise, Macy, Maddie and myself. This would be the most upsetting to Louise out of all I had done. She's my life, my best friend. She was the only mum I ever had. But the magnet in me continued to attract only my feelings, repelling others creeping in.

The unpredictability of the scenario was weighing on my mind. Anybody could have written the letter. I couldn't go alone. Of course, Victoria and Bea would have been my first option, but friendship had faded. I isolated myself with only them, and now I was alone to repair the damage they caused.

Sam worked in the chip shop after school. Before Victoria and Bea, I'd join him every day, ordering as much as I could so we could spend hours laughing together. I became oblivious to my friendship with

Sam because I wanted Victoria and Bea to acknowledge me. And now I wish they hadn't.

A queue of people had started to gather and was growing by the minute. Sam wasn't at the counter; nobody was. It was unlike him to be late as he would set alarms to avoid confrontation with his boss. People in the line began to grow impatient. A tall, tattooed man began to tantrum.

"I've been waiting for over 20 minutes now! Is someone there?"

A distant Sam emerged from behind the glass food display, drained of energy. The brief moment of eye contact pinched my heart, triggering water to my tear ducts. As the shop began to empty, Sam took orders slower, breathing deeper each time he handed change to the customer. Until there were only two of us left.

"Hi, could I have-"

"Why did you do it, Mel?"

Sam's question left me stunned. He fixed his gaze on me, and I felt myself in his shoes for the first time since last term. Despite all attempts to repair the damage, they still remained broken. The decision to shorten the disrupted shoelaces was never his own. I was the most significant break, torn from his ankle to his toe, with the last thread ripping as we spoke. The truth was, I didn't have a reason that justified everything. Always ready to point the finger at others when it was my fault. Every phrase that came to mind was meaningless, and I knew he wasn't interested in what I had to say. I proceeded through tears, ignoring the question.

"I think I'll just have chips."

As he moved his eyes, two droplets of tears landed on the cash register. Then, he returned my gaze. I braced myself for the worst.

"I forgive you."

People in class heard what Bea revealed. They all flooded Sam with kindness during lesson change. He thanked me. I didn't deserve it.

"I didn't hide it because I'm ashamed. I just wasn't mentally ready for anybody's opinion on my life."

It wasn't my secret to reveal. We locked eyes, both experiencing the healing of the other. Then, a middle-aged man with receding, dyed black hair stormed out of the shop's rear rooms.

"So first you're late, and now this? Be careful Sam; you won't have a job anymore!"

Sam turned to me and grinned.

"Don't worry, mate, I quit."

Then, he threw his apron on the floor and reached for my hand. We squeezed our way through the queue of people that had now gathered outside the shop, racing as fast as our legs could carry us.

We came to a halt outside the park, and I realised I was yet to tell Sam anything.

"There's something I need to ask you." I handed the folded letter and walked in front as he read it.

"So, you're here to meet your apparent Dad?"

I didn't like how Sam said apparent; it sounded like he believed the letter was fake. Sam cut me off before I could respond.

"Now?"

He grabbed the same hand and propelled me back into running. I hadn't had time to feel nervous about Dad. I wanted to remove my high expectations for an ideal father figure. But he had never been to prison, so how bad of a person could he be?

The deserted park made me thankful for Sam. Then, as everything began to process, I realised how huge of a mistake this could be.

"Have you got a ligh'er?"

A husky voice from behind startled both Sam and me.

"Oh, don't worry, I found one."

The voice belonged to a bald man who looked to be in his late fifties. We observed as he struggled to light his cigarette, which was balanced between his fingers. Mud had caked his wet jeans, and his burgundy woollen jumper appeared to have stretched out over time. Clouds of cigarette smoke gathered at the corners of his lips. A sudden buzz of Sam's phone caught all our attention. I noticed him angling the phone screen away from me.

"Oh Mel, my mum's texting me."

Three more buzzes followed."A lot. I'm sorry, I'm gonna 'ave to leave ya."

He gestured his head to the bald man, who was still puffing cigarette smoke. I nodded, assuring him I'd be safe.

"Text me minute-by-minute updates, alright?"

I nodded once more. Fearing being alone, I watched Sam run through the park gate. But he was part of my life again, and that's all that mattered.

"Is that your boyfriend?"

The man's husky voice appeared again. I didn't expect to hear it again. Still, he was standing so close to me.

"No, no. Just a very close friend." I forced a laugh.

The man licked his thumb and index finger and put out his cigarette.

"Shame, he's a good-looking lad. Would've given me great grandkids."

I paused in my thoughts and repeated the statement he spoke three times in my head. Louise had always maintained my dad was the same age as Mum; this man was ancient. My heart sank. There were only three possibilities: His deception had me on the verge of death, or he was confused and needed help. I wouldn't allow the third to enter my thoughts.

"S'kay, Milly, I'm not gonna eat ya. I'm glad you came. I thought that bitch Louise would 'ave stopped ya."

He had to stop speaking. Every sentence blurred all forms of logic in my head. I had never known a Milly, and Louise could have easily been a coincidence.

"Louise?" I questioned, purposely giving no details of my life with my reply.

"Yeah, My sister-in-law? Your aunt? Come on, you are on this planet, aren't ya?" He grinned.

It confirmed what I thought I wanted. He's my dad? *My* dad? He could answer the questions that had stayed unanswered all my life. The father figure that had been absent had re-appeared. I pushed aside the brief disappointment and the name he gave Louise and opened my arms for the hug I'd been waiting for since I was young. But Dad appeared uninterested, so I shamefully dropped my arms.

"No, um look. I need to ask you something," Dad stuttered.

I began to justify his response in my head. Why would he want a hug from me? I barely spoke a word to him. But despite my willingness to apologise, I didn't. Dad was beginning to get impatient with the pauses between each question he asked. Although I was positive he was my dad, I was hesitant to say any more.

"So, I lost a lot of my money on a bet, so bring money to me in the same place tomorrow."

This time it wasn't a question, it was a statement, and it crushed me. I became engrossed in a stupid fantasy, resulting in my hope shattering in seconds.

Silence.

My airways began closing as I ran further away. The cry I howled echoed down the lonely streets. The clouds began to weep as I stood outside Louise's house, anticipating the arrival of bags of my belongings to greet me. This time Louise would know the truth, and no more secrets would be kept from her. The door opened with a click, but my eyes were fixed on the ground. Eventually, I was able to raise my head. Louise opened her arms before my eyes reached her face. The hug that had been with me all my life. I dropped my bag to the side and squeezed her tighter than ever.

"I had hoped, too, that he was different, that he changed. But don't worry my sweet, you have me. You will always have me."

She hugged me tighter.

"Your friend Sam phoned and told me about the letter."

In the shock of Dad, I forgot the updates I meant to give Sam. I halted my anger, seeing his worry before I felt betrayed. Louise put her palms on my cheeks and tilted my head until my eyes met hers.

"Sam told me one more thing."

It was difficult for me to not assume the worst. The day re-winded and my movements and conversations raced through my brain, looking for a fault. It was too unclear for a definite mistake. But what Louise told me was far worse than a false movement.

Sam was never returning.

Chapter Five
Faith

The car's rear-view mirror reflected Mum's frustration. It appeared the moment Ethan and I arrived back from the café. Returning to the old town achieved what I thought would be enough for Mum. My health was excellent and the dreaded hospital trips were no longer needed. There wasn't a way I could live up to her high expectations. In the mirror I studied her expressions, moving my eyes anytime I came in contact with hers. Avoiding sensitive subjects meant we didn't speak a word to each other. My sexuality had crept back into my mind, and pushing it out created another worry. Even though I needed to contact Melissa for updates on the school project, I couldn't persuade Mum to let me have a phone.

"I didn't have a phone until I was much older than you, and—"

The same sentence would never finish, constantly dissolving before the end. I needed to ask what followed, why certain words never reached the air. But the risk of breaking Mum was too high.

A precise eeriness appeared as we entered Dawnton. It was stronger. I saw Mum feel it too. Driving past the sign was enough to stop any conversation that had begun.

As we drove closer to our house, the gaps between the trees caught my attention. A view of our front window had come into sight, but a head disrupted the direct view onto the fireplace. His head was barely recognisable enough to figure out it was Dad. His motions were frantic and I wondered if he heard the car driving near, since I was sure the time we were arriving home had no way of reaching him. Mum wouldn't give the time to anybody as the anxiety of coming later than expected was unbearable to her. As our car turned into the drive, Dad moved out of sight.

Each of Mum's bones tensed up as we left the car. Then, finally, the front door unlocked and Mum screamed a cry into Dad's arms. I froze in terror.

"Was everything okay with her?"

Dad's voice began to crack. He comforted her head as it lay on his chest.

"Yes, everything is great with her health. But she didn't remember anything, Eric!"

"Don't be silly, Jan. She has her health. That's all that matters."

Dad's words felt kinder to my heart.

"To live a great life, she doesn't need to live by what she remembers. So let it go, Janice."

Though still by the car, I felt the breath she exhaled. Letting go of the old me would give the peace we had been both searching for. As she turned her head towards me, sorrow shone in her eyes.

Mum needed the space to heal. As did I.

My bedroom would be where I was completely alone with my thoughts, so I spent the least of my time there. I knew the dull brown décor of the room would inevitably lower my mood, and there hadn't been a night where I slept the whole way through. I wondered if my air mattress was becoming a permanent part of the furniture. Every thought I had was exhausting, so the mattress seemed to start appealing more.

I'd feel better tomorrow, I thought, as I laid my head on my pillow.

My reality started to drift into empty dreams.

All of a sudden, something jolted me awake. I began hearing a familiar voice emerging from the light, repeating over.

"Better."

"Better."

"Better."

Better? I couldn't begin the process of understanding. They needed me to recognise the words, and I felt the urgency.

"Better."

"Better."

"Help her!"

It finally was clear.

"Help who?!" I shouted. Magically, the light faded. As time began ticking again, the pain in my chest amplified. The weeks waiting for a memory to reappear in my brain felt different from what I anticipated. But it didn't feel like this was a past recollection. There was a purpose to those words.

"I'll tuck you in."

Mum must have heard me shout from her room. There was rare peaceful energy coated around her body. She tucked each corner of my blanket under me and lightly kissed my forehead.

"I'm so sorry, Faith. I'm getting the help I need. I promise."

I was absent from school again the next day. Mum thought it would benefit us all if we took a day out to unpack everything. There was a feeling of doubt as I removed my sixth makeup bag from the box. Mum assured me everything within the box belonged to me but it all felt far from who I was.

The house phone had begun to collect a stack of voicemails, all left by the same number. The number developed into a face when a frustrated man arrived at our house in overalls, holding bags of paintbrushes. I expected him to start the much-needed decorating but Mum ended his perseverance.

"You're at the wrong house. You have made a mistake. Stop bothering us!"

Dad didn't phone for any other services after that, leaving the painting and decorating for us all to do alone. But it relieved the worry that Mum and Dad's idea for my room décor was being influenced by my old self.

With most of the money spent on the people working on the house, the decorating had to wait. Watching Dad attempt to fit boxes into the kitchen cupboards sparked my curiosity about what the house actually held. I had only ventured into a handful of the rooms, and I figured the time in the day would move faster if I had something to do.

Outside my room was a hook attached to a short pole sitting under a small square door on the roof. I slotted the hook onto the latch and pulled it open. A ladder shot past me, crashing onto the ground. I stood motionless in the silence that followed, expecting to hear footsteps running up the stairs. But there were none. It was the reassurance I needed to go up there.

An unblemished mahogany display cabinet stood out among it all. I picked up the box closest to me and pulled out a discoloured lavender blouse. The style, I was sure, revealed it belonged to an elderly woman. Each blouse, neatly folded beneath, had the same shade but with varied stitched floral designs on the collar. I assumed the other boxes held more clothing and wondered why they were being crammed in the attic to collect dust. I needed to know who she was. No other boxes were within reaching distance, so the only option was to climb in.

Dust heavily coated all the boxes. All except two.

The first box was full of old handwritten letters, all addressed to a woman named Betty. The tiny joint-up writing had faded, making them difficult to read. As I took the letters out, a corner of one appeared from the middle of the pile. The only one in blue ink.

'To my dearest Betty,

I have missed you ever so much today. I boxed up a few more of your dresses. I know you told me to throw it all away, but I can't. Not yet. I've managed to keep myself strong for Jan. My love for you has never been stronger, but my world has never been lonelier. Why couldn't it have been me? You didn't deserve to die. I know when you visit me. I feel you; I promise I do.

All my love, Ted.'

I closed the box. It didn't feel right to continue reading them.

Next to my arm was the second box and at first glance I didn't notice it was smaller. In large letters at the top were the words *'family photographs.'* I opened it and picked up the first photo. It was an older man sitting on a deckchair, holding a newspaper. I turned the image over to see 'Ted White 60th birthday' written in tiny writing on the back.

"White?" I whispered to myself.

The familiarity caused me to search through my brain for the names of people I had met.

"Janice White!"

Everything started to fall into place. Ted was my granddad and his death must have been why Mum found moving to the house so difficult, why she couldn't change his decor. I flicked through the following several photographs expecting to recognise myself, but I couldn't. Most photos were black and white, and many featured a younger Mum and Dad. Then, a photo of a brown shotgun sitting in a display cabinet came to the top of the pile. I flipped the image over to see if there was a purpose for it to be in with the rest of the family photos. Someone had over-written what was there before. The words were uneven, and it was clear by seeing his letters that Ted took pride in his handwriting. I focused my attention more.

"MY LETTER WAS FOUND. RUN AS FAR AWAY AS POSSIBLE."

A crucifying pain appeared in my chest, causing me to collapse. I could do nothing. Telling Mum would cause her stress to rise again. A call from downstairs travelled into the attic.

"Dinner!"

I noticed Mum wipe droplets of pasta sauce from the plate's outer circle before she brought it over to the table. I felt the effort she was putting in for us all and I wondered if each day before my coma would have mimicked this.

Knowing how fast I could eat without Mum thinking I would prefer to be elsewhere was difficult. What I found in the attic captivated my brain and I needed to see what else was up there.

Once I finished, I slowly walked out of the room and waited until I was out of sight to run up the stairs.

Desperately, I looked through the same box of photos, hoping to find another with the same ink, hoping it was a part of some bizarre board game. What I thought I had discovered had become clouded. Mum never held back on the stories of events or party's that we all celebrated. Her words matched the pictures, yet, I was missing. I grabbed the picture of the shotgun again, realising I recognised what the gun was sitting on. The mahogany display cabinet. Tiptoeing around the boxes became a challenge. Understandably, the gun wasn't on display; it would be easy for someone to take it. But the cupboard didn't hold it either.

Without warning, footsteps appeared from the ladder. My heart jumped as I realised there was no time to place the picture back in the box. Thankfully, it wasn't Mum's face that came into sight. It was Dads. He moved his glance down to the picture I was holding.

"Put that away!" He shouted under his breath.

It confused me since I didn't have hold of an actual gun.

"Don't let your mother see!"

Granddad's own gun killed him. He missed his Betty so much so I assumed it was suicide. But I had no way to confirm and Dad wouldn't tell me anything else.

"Him dying was bad enough, but then you fell into a coma." Dad's eyes became strong, "I nearly lost her."

"Where's the gun now?"

My voice was faster than my thoughts. But regret wasn't the first emotion that came to mind.

For the first time, Dad raised his voice and yelled at me to go to bed. The heavy ache in my chest was beginning to reappear, so it was difficult to feel upset at his anger.

I would never go up to the attic again. And I believed myself for a while...

Chapter Six
Melissa

P laying pretend was the only way to cure my loneliness when I was young. The game 'Mummies and Daddies' worked the best with a Mum who was five and a dad who was five and a half. Any tears from an argument would disappear once somebody bigger mended the harm. There was never a moment where I felt forgotten. I feared falling back into that same emptiness I felt as a child, knowing that the game of pretend wouldn't be enough anymore. I was being left behind by everybody I once knew, a memory they would soon forget. How long until Louise and the twins would leave as well?

Howls of laughter were reaching my room from Macy and Maddie's. I stepped across the landing, hoping they wouldn't hear my footsteps. But, as I got to the edge of the door frame, Louise caught sight of me and gestured her head for me to join them.

"Maddie, do you want to give it to her now?" Louise asked.

Maddie hopped out of bed and ran towards a pink sparkly painted box. She pulled out a piece of paper and held it close to her chest, squinting her eyes to be sure I couldn't see it.

"I wrote you a poem, Mel!"

And just like that, the void I felt had started to fill.

"Mel gives me joy,

47

She brings me lots of toys,
When I see her sad,
I want to give her some back,
Because she's the best sister ever,
And so, so so clever,
I want to see her happy again,
Because she's my bestest friend."

My family was already here. Louise had always been the person to mend the harm from my game of 'Mummies and Daddies.' I'd wasted years of my life wishing for my parents. Louise, Macy and Maddie would forever be here, and I wished I realised it sooner.

Maddie seemed concerned as she finished reading her poem.

"They are happy tears, I promise!" I assured her.

I left their room to let Louise wish them goodnight.

I couldn't remember much after. Louise's stories to the twins also seemed to have helped me sleep that night.

My heart sunk with dread as I awoke. I attempted to mask it with the excitement of Faith returning to school. Still, I knew I needed to stop suppressing every complex emotion I felt. My new life and perspective were to start today, and I was to begin with the ignored messages from Sam. It was becoming selfish, and I had been on the other end of selfishness too much to be doing it to someone else.

It relieved me to hear his phone go straight to voice mail.

"Hi Sam, um..."

The words that once flowed when speaking to him had frozen. I felt the grief root in my heart as Louise told me how far away he had moved. But our new chapters were beginning and we had to be there for each other.

"No matter how far away you are from me, I will always be there for you. I love you."

The time it took to travel to school in the car wouldn't have been enough to gather my thoughts and push them to the back of my head. Walking barely allowed it to happen.

At the front gate stood a line of pupils smirking as I walked through. It was challenging to guide myself away from over-thinking. Still, I managed to clear my head and continued to walk into the schoolyard. Disgusted faces with piercing eyes were scanning me head to toe. Groups of whispers surrounded me, and yet my heartbeat was the loudest sound out of it all. To filter out the words from the giggles and gasps would mean I would have to face what they knew, so I let it all fade together. I should have trusted my gut. Victoria and Bea prepared from the beginning to destroy me. They just waited to begin the humiliation.

A sudden yell was loud enough for me to hear over the circle of laughter. The first lesson bell rang in time to discover whose voice it was. Gabriella Lucas remained in front of Victoria and Bea. Her anger radiated out of her skin. She scrunched her fingers together and lifted her arm to be parallel to their faces. Then, Gabriella took a glance at me and immediately dropped her arm.

She darted in my direction. Thoughts began scrolling through my brain, trying to discover what created such anger and why it was aimed at me.

"Mel! Are you okay?"

It took a while for my mind and body to connect again. The words Gabriella spoke were in slow motion, so I wasn't sure if my brain was being delayed by a punch.

"They are the worst two people I have ever encountered, pure evil. So don't take any notice of what they say, Mel."

I had never seen such a kind and open side to Gabriella. Once she formed a friendship with Victoria and Bea, she became cruel. I couldn't hold much trust in the words she spoke.

"Do you remember when I was friends with them? I transformed myself into a perfect clone. Everything's fine until you do something they don't like, and then they try to ruin your life."

She brought forward memories of an endless list of girls that had become the third friend to Victoria and Bea. Throughout the years, several of the girls left Dawnton High when the bullying became overbearing. When they offer the empty third space to you, rose-tinted curtains cover the hurt they printed on others before and you can accept yourself to become one of them. Gabriella went into detail about the years she was with them and I began to notice it felt very familiar to me.

Gabriella wanted to make sure I was aware of the most important thing. Victoria and Bea keep a secret that they don't think will elicit a strong enough reaction. Then they fabricate a lie, forcing you to admit the true secret.

"The lie they told of me was that naked photo I had supposedly sent. And you see, it's still a rumour around school because I'm not giving them the power of forcing me to reveal something I don't want to."

I began to become anxious that the lie they had about me was the truth. Victoria and Bea wouldn't need to fabricate anything if the actual secret would have a strong enough reaction. Gabriella began asking questions about the rumour.

"I would rather not know the lie they have on me for as long as possible," I stressed.

Nobody had ever been brave enough to ask someone directly, so I felt safe for the time being.

I was naive to assume Faith would ignore the rumours. My brain singled her out as I walked into English, noticing her deliberate attempt to force me away. There was no other explanation for why she sat in my chair that day. I should have been numb to the pain of loss, yet this was almost as severe as when Sam left. The only other empty chair was where he once sat. Knowing our neglected friendship was because I chose to prioritise Victoria and Bea over him, kept causing my heart to ache. I wasn't ready to convince Faith to continue working with me on the project, so I went and sat in Sam's chair.

I managed to not pull the attention of many as I walked in, so the whispers in class felt less than in the schoolyard. Faith flicked her glossy hair behind her shoulder, slightly turning her head in my direction.

"Melissa!"

Her entire face lifted as she walked toward me.

"You're not in the group anymore."

My hope blurred with the words she spoke. I couldn't figure out what had enticed Faith to fall into their trap. But I knew there wouldn't need to be one if the truth was being spread across the school.

"Melissa?"

My heart crumbled the longer she stood in front of me. I couldn't bring myself to glance up at her again. I desperately wanted to get out of the school and out of Dawnton.

"Mrs Beckett said we can be in a group with just the two of us."

I waited in the seconds after Faith spoke, waiting for Victoria and Bea to begin the dominos of laughter. Bea moved her needle eyes onto us, and my trust for Faith diminished. Victoria bellowed a laugh, echoed by the class. Students walking past heard her and crowded by the door. Running away wasn't an option anymore.

The world detached and started to spin before me. A flood of darkness engulfed my mind.

"Shut up! All of you!"

Faith's voice. Her hand pulled me out of my chair. She guided me through the still classroom and brought me to the corridor. The students who had gathered at the door had dispersed through the hall. Faith wrapped her arms around me.

"Their group project idea was awful anyway."

I couldn't understand why she was so kind to me.

We both heard the sound of heels approaching us. Mrs Beckett's foot dragged slightly each time she made a step, so I knew it was her.

"Sorry girls, I had a hectic morning! I had no idea Sam moved schools."

Faith was unaware too. She turned to me and waited for my reaction, but I kept my eyes on Mrs Beckett. I knew she was still unsure of what caused my friendship with Sam to end, and I was still hesitant to tell her. Since we began working together, the thought of losing Faith was unbearable to me. Something about her made me feel whole, a feeling of familiarity. It was as if I had known her my entire life.

"What are you both doing out here?" Mrs Beckett's tone had changed.

I had yet to be successful with a believable lie that was strong enough for Mrs Beckett to let me leave her class. She had the frustrating ability to detect a lie before it was said.

"I'm not feeling well, so I'm going home," Faith said.

Before I could even try, it was over. But I didn't blame Faith for not realising how strict Mrs Beckett was about people leaving class. It appeared that it became much more challenging after the incident that changed our town. I was preparing to run because I couldn't return to class. Mrs Beckett gave me a glance.

"I also wanted Melissa accompanying me in case anything terrible happened."

Mrs Beckett nodded and moved to the side to let us pass without hesitation. I wondered if everyone felt the same way I did about Faith because this was not the teacher I knew.

Her voice followed us as we walked past.

"Try to come up with a new project idea, girls."

It felt strange to leave school early while the teachers were aware of my whereabouts. So often I'd have to plan a way out and persuade someone to cover for me. Faith was, I suppose, my cover for the day. As we stepped out the front gates, the suffocation I was experiencing had vanished. We came to a halt, unsure of what to do next.

"Where should we go?" Faith asked.

I felt relieved as she asked me. I didn't want Faith to feel obligated to stay with me, but I also didn't want to wander the streets alone.

"I don't know my way around here yet," Faith added.

I was still afraid she would reveal the secret that everybody knew about me, so I needed to be sure to keep the conversation away from what had happened.

"The parks aren't far away; we can just walk around," I stated.

We began walking on the path that led away from the school, and it occurred to me how easily Mrs Beckett had let Faith go. There were so many specific details of Faith's life that I never understood. I was still uncertain about why she only stayed at school for an hour or why the teachers acted differently when she was nearby. The accidental silence between Faith and I had grown deafeningly loud. I had a strong desire to learn more about her. She was wonderful to me, but we would have to share more about ourselves if we were to work together. I needed to know what she was hiding.

Chapter Seven
Faith

I was unsure if I should have interrupted the gradual silence that began to grow between us. I could see how deeply Melissa had lost herself in her thoughts, and I didn't want to say something that would hurt her further. There were moments in the lesson when I would sense she was struggling outside of school. I recognised her behaviours when processing hurt, but it never felt right to ask.

There was no reason to justify how cruel people had been towards Melissa, and it seemed I wasn't the only one who thought it that morning. Until recently, I only knew of Gabriella Lucas through a conveyor belt of rumours spoken around the school. She stood outside the school gates, gnawing at her fingernails. Her gaze flew from student to student as they walked through, halting her eyes when she saw me.

"Faith?"

I had no idea she knew who I was.

"Don't listen to what they are saying about Mel."

There was one rumour that I knew to be true about Gabriella; she and Melissa were never friends. Being the new student at Dawnton High made me vulnerable to falling for lies so I felt reluctant to believe her, fearing this was a way to harm Melissa through me.

"Stay by her. She will need you."

Uneasiness climbed through her body. She turned away and hurried through the school gates. I was at a loss for what to do and became irritated that Mum was so adamant about me not having a phone.

I hoped for the possibility that Melissa had already arrived at school. I dashed over to the English block, wishing to see a glimpse of her. But as I stepped into the classroom, not even Mrs Beckett was there. A sticky note on her desk fluttered from the breeze, drawing my attention.

'New Groups;
Victoria & Bea, Melissa & Faith'

I felt selfish to feel happy about the group being Melissa and me, not knowing what caused the decision. But if the group change resulted from whatever had happened with Melissa, I wanted her to see that she still had me.

"I guess we could use this time to be productive anyway," I voiced, knowing I had to break the silence that formed between us at some point.

Melissa's thoughts were still absorbing her. I never got the chance to ask what had happened while I was away. Even the current silence didn't tempt me to ask questions. I made the decision not to bring it up until she chose to. Bringing the conversation back to a neutral state was the best thing to do.

"Why don't you list some things you're interested in, and we could attempt to morph it into persuasive writing," I added.

Melissa's face brightened.

"What interests you?" She questioned.

It was surprising how she bounced back at me from what I said. My wrong choice of words again landed me in a situation I regretted. I felt so detached from the previous self that I knew I couldn't use that knowledge to talk myself out. In a panic, I responded.

"I'm not sure; you go first."

Melissa came to a halt, causing me to do the same. She took a step in front and turned herself to face me. She placed her hands on the top of both of my arms.

"Look, Faith, you don't have to hide anything from me, my life is a wreck, and everyone already hates me; I won't judge you."

I'd never seen her be so direct. When the questions begin about my life, I shrink and stumble over my words, each time noticing Melissa becoming confused and, more recently, frustrated. She wouldn't judge me; I believed that. There was a trust with her that I had not experienced with anybody else before. But I just didn't feel ready to tell my truth.

Melissa's hands dropped from my arms.

"Faith, I'm so sorry."

Her head lowered in shame. For a long time, I was afraid of overstepping boundaries. I never asked about her home life; why did she feel entitled to know about mine? I let her wallow in her conscience.

"I don't know why I do things like that," Melissa added.

She had moved a foot away and was staring into the road. I watched her hand brush through her hair. Maybe the truth was inevitable now that we'd work so closely together. At that moment, it seemed right to tell her.

"I don't know is the answer to every question. I have no idea who I am or how to live up to the expectations that others have of me."

I noticed Melissa approaching closer to me through the blurriness of my now tear-filled eyes. I felt the comfort of her hands as she placed them back on my arms.

"Who do people expect you to be?" She asked, her eyebrows dipping.

I hadn't realised how built up my emotions had become over the weeks of being at home because as she asked, I burst into tears. To keep Mum from breaking again, I had no other option but to keep quiet about how I felt. There wasn't anybody I felt close enough to talk to because my family still felt so distant. Melissa was different. With her, I felt at ease.

"The girl I was before the coma," I cried.

Melissa wrapped her arms around me, and I sobbed for what seemed like forever. She began sniffling too. It was something we both needed. She gently pushed me back and tilted my head to wipe my tears away.

"You don't have to tell me anymore here, or even at all," Melissa said.

She took my arm in hers, and we began walking again.

"We should talk about something a bit more light-hearted," she grins.

We both gazed up at each other, triggering unexpected laughter. It was exhausting to begin to process what happened that day and the laughter relieved some of the stress.

Something was attracting Melissa's attention away, causing her to unlink from my arm. I worried the same feelings that she felt in English class were returning.

"How about convincing we can solve unsolvable crimes?" Melissa said.

I followed the direction of her glance to a parked police car sitting at the corner of the road. I didn't want her to lose the sudden enthusiasm so I agreed, not knowing where to begin. Melissa seemed eager to get started as soon as possible.

"Since I can't go home, the park bench will have to be our station. Do you get it? Station?" Chuckled Melissa.

I giggled. It felt amazing to see Melissa become herself again.

"Or we could go to my house?" I replied.

My response seemed to shock her. I figured it would be the most effective way for her to know more about my life without having to say anything else. My only worry was knowing Mum would be home. There hadn't been a conversation about bringing home friends, and I was unsure how she would react.

I felt discomfort when walking up the path to my house, similar to the first time I arrived at our old house from the hospital. The feeling of the unknown. It had been present but slight as the weeks went by, and I assumed I was adjusting to home life with a family that I didn't know existed. But there had been a new shift after being with Melissa, and I kept checking to see if I had arrived at the wrong house. I thought the day must have taken a more profound toll on me than expected. I looked at Melissa, and she looked in shock.

"Your house is huge!"

It was. Most of it I still hadn't discovered. It was my home, yet I didn't feel settled enough to unpack my life.

The front door was unlatched as we were walking closer. I had hoped it not to be Mum, but sure enough, it was. Her forced smile turned to panic as she noticed Melissa.

"Mum, this is a friend from school. We're working on a project together," I said, hoping Melissa didn't notice Mum's change in mood.

Dad appeared from the side of the house holding gardening tools.

"Oh, hello, come in! What's your name?"

Mum forcefully pulled back her panic and moved aside to let us in.

"Melissa."

I picked up the worried whispers from Mum as Melissa and I walked through. I thought it would be difficult for Mum to let someone new into granddad's house, but her main concern was whether she had cooked enough to feed an extra person. As part of her healing, Mum decided to cook dinner for the family every night. Each evening, she prepared the ingredients for the number of people eating. Suppose the recipe fed seven, and three of us were eating, Mum would begin her precise calculations to be sure there's never anything over.

I brought Melissa through the hallway and stairs, guiding her through the obstacle course of boxes.

"Sorry, we haven't had a chance to unpack."

For a brief moment, I felt a disconnect in my sight. With each step I took, it felt like I was dragging myself out of an overlap of Melissa's sight. As if for that moment, whatever she saw was bleeding into my vision. It wasn't a sensation I had felt before, but the days stress, I knew, was to blame.

I felt a rise in embarrassment as we reached my room. It had stayed the same since we moved in because there hadn't been an opportunity to make it my own. I walked to my desk chair to avoid seeing Melissa's reaction.

"Can I sit on here?" She asked.

Seeing her stand in front of my air mattress startled me. I nodded, unsure how I could explain what had happened with Mum.

Melissa stared at the ceiling and then at each corner of my room. I worried she felt uneasy.

"Faith, can you come down here for a second." I wasn't alarmed by Dad's tone of voice.

I saw Dad's arm soothe Mum as I walked into the kitchen. This time I didn't want to hear it. She promised she was getting the help she needed. Having a friend over shouldn't cause such an upset. Everything had to run through Mum to see if she could handle it, and when she couldn't, I would feel the guilt of attempting to have a regular life or ask normal questions. I didn't want to live that way anymore.

"You're going to have to ask Melissa to leave."

Chapter Eight
Melissa

"Your mother isn't ready to have someone around."

"But why? I thought she was getting help for it all!"

"She can come for dinner at the end of the week, we will free up the day, and your mother will have time to prepare everything."

"She wasn't even here for dinner!"

Creaks followed the footsteps that ran up the stairs. My thoughts weaved within the words Faith's dad spoke; oddly, I didn't feel offended. It sparked a further curiosity about Faith's life and I wondered if there was something that once happened at a family dinner. I hoped she wouldn't notice I overheard but letting her hold the pressure of repeating it back to me felt unfair. So, as she entered the room, I told her a believable lie to leave.

"The school has contacted my aunt about what happened today."

Faith's face had become sunken from her fighting back the tears.

"She's so worried, and I think I should go home to tell her I'm okay," I added.

Faith returned to her desk chair without saying a thing. I worried my guilt caused a recognisable tone that uncovered it was a lie.

"I don't know how I'll ever repay you for what you did for me today. Thank you," I continued.

Faith saved my life. And if she wasn't there, I don't know what would have happened to me. Faith's expression brightened and her shoulders loosened. I wrapped my arms around her to help ensure I didn't mind having to go. She exhaled a deep sigh. As we released from hugging, I noticed a pen and notepad on the desk in front of her, reminding me of a thought I had earlier in the day.

"My address. If you ever need me for something." It was the quickest way she could contact me without having a phone.

As I made my way down the stairs, I noticed every box had been re-positioned to the kitchen. Faith's mum sat slouched on the dining chair. As I walked by, she smiled.

"Bye, darling."

Her voice was kind but exhausted, and my confusion with having to leave fell to empathy. She seemed so fragile.

The possibility of the school actually contacting Louise had started to latch onto my thoughts. It would still be school hours when I returned home, and I worried that telling her the day's events would cause stress. But I had made a promise and I intended to keep it. Unfortunately, Louise was pottering in the front garden, leaving me no time to prepare my words.

"Why are you home so early?"

I assumed I'd be able to keep my composure while telling her everything. But the overwhelming rush of emotion shattered my peaceful demeanour. She rushed over to me, pulling off her gardening gloves.

"Oh, Mel! Come on in, I'll put the kettle on, and you can tell me what's happened."

For the next couple of days, I was absent from school. Louise assured me I could take as much time off as needed, and she would deal with any consequence. School had never felt like a chore for me. I always found myself at the top of every class, flooded with praise from the teachers. My main passion was English and when Faith entered our class, I became even more captivated by the subject. However, I wasn't sure if I could ever recover from what Victoria and Bea did. Louise encouraged me to seal the trauma from that day into a capsule in my brain and to only revisit it when the pain had passed. I tried, but it was still all I thought of.

There was a call from Louise to come downstairs. Milo had been finding new methods to reach the food I forgot to put away, so I dashed down the stairs, hoping to stop him from devouring more than he already had. I halted as I noticed somebody standing at the front door. I was apprehensive about seeing who it was, knowing I wasn't prepared to speak with my teachers, or worse, Victoria and Bea. I tilted my head. It was Faith. Relief covered my anxieties.

"Here she is." Louise walked over to the bottom of the stairs.

"Are you feeling well enough to let her come in?" She whispered.

"Yeah." Saying more would make it too obvious it was seeing Faith that caused me to feel better.

Milo sprung out of nowhere, catching Faith's face with his lick as she walked in.

"Wow! He's usually so timid with new people." Louise, surprised, started laughing.

The fire drill at school came to mind. Faith recognised Milo by name but was yet to explain to me how. There was a creeping assumption that had begun to cut through my thoughts. It was near unthinkable, but it would explain how she knew Milo.

"I think she might know him. She knew his name when he escaped that day," I said, wondering if she would tell her reason now.

Faith was overcome by panic.

"I think I heard someone mention your dog in school."

I pushed the horrific thought further back into my mind. Trusting Faith was easier than losing somebody else I cared so much for.

"Well, you should feel very flattered," Louise replied, breaking the tense atmosphere. "Mel, show her to the living room; I've got to go and pick up the twins from school now."

With it being Faith and me, the worry that she was here because of another horrible instant at school had climbed to the forefront of my mind. I knew it had to be the first thing I asked.

"What brought you here?"

Faith moved her focus away from the sofa. "You weren't at school again, so I wanted to ensure you were okay."

I took a seat on the sofa, realising her heavy focus was probably due to her wanting to do the same. Our persuasive writing project had reached a standstill, and I felt responsible for lowering her end-of-school grade. It was the only lesson she was at school for, and she had never spoken about any work she did at home. The school gates plagued my dreams and left me unsure if I would ever return. Guilt hung heavily on my shoulders.

"I'm okay," I falsely replied. "You didn't need to waste your school time to come and check on me, though." I responded with a smile, showing I appreciated that she did.

"I've finished my classes for today; besides, I never got the chance to invite you for dinner this evening."

She increased the pitch of her voice, "but don't feel obliged to come; it's just a dinner my mum has planned."

The lack of pressure seemed unconvincing. It was difficult to forget the conversation I overheard between Faith and her dad at their house. So I just continued to leave the approaching dinner buried beneath more stressful thoughts.

"I'll be there."

Faith lifted her posture as she noticed the clock.

"I'll meet you at my house in an hour, don't be late!" She exclaimed as she began making her way to the front door.

She paused and glanced back with an uneasy smile. "Or early."

I was early. But only by minutes. I waited out of sight of the front-facing windows of Faith's house, left unsure how serious her last remarks were. I watched the minutes pass on my watch, leaving it to the final seconds to walk up the front drive. The door was unlatched before I could knock, and Faith's mum came into sight.

"Hello, Melissa! Welcome to our home. She gestured her arm for me to walk in. "I have just set the table, so you get the first choice of where to sit!"

Enthusiasm held the place of the fragile woman I saw slouched on the dining chair. She greeted me with such warmth, which was a surprise.

Folded napkins sat on top of aligned dinner plates. Besides them, three ascending silver forks and spoons mirrored the flame of two centrepiece candles. Only in restaurants had I seen that style of crockery before. Faith's mum gathered serving spoons and placed them on the table. She tilted her head towards the ceiling.

"Dinners ready!"

The stairs creaked with a sudden rumble. Faith's dad was the first to enter the kitchen.

"Oh, hello Melissa, I didn't know you had arrived!"

Immediately followed by Faith.

"Melissa? Mum, you didn't tell me she was here!" Faith appeared relieved after she saw me.

The conversation fell empty as soon as everybody sat down to eat.

"I love how you set out the table, um..." I wasn't sure if calling her Mrs Mathews would be too formal. Or if it was even her who set the table.

"Look at us; we haven't even told you our names!" Faith's mum enthused.

She placed her hand on her chest.

"I'm Janice, and this is—"

"Eric," Faith's dad interrupted.

Janice didn't seem fazed that he did.

"I was overjoyed once I knew Faith had made a friend, and it's lovely to finally meet you."

I grinned, assuming the frail way I saw her last time made her pretend it had never happened. I looked over to Faith, noticing her locked gaze on me shifting as our eyes met. She and Eric's lack of reaction to Janice's words were surprising, and once again paused the conversation. But Faith's unprovoked stare was not a one-time thing. I'd get glimpses of her out of my eye and then catch her head turning away when I returned the stare. I began to fear the worse and felt desperate to move the attention away from me. Once again, feeling responsible for starting the conversation.

"You're lucky that the wild rabbits come right up to the window."

There was a continuous view through the house and into the back garden. It wasn't like Louise's place; Milo would frighten any wildlife away before they got close for a start.

"They come out every morning and evening," Janice replied in delight. "Dawn and dusk, the hunt is a must, my father used to say."

Eric paused, mid-chew.

"Hunt?" It was the first time Faith had spoken since she greeted me.

"Your Grandfather used to love to shoot. His father taught him as a boy and tried to teach me, but," she giggled, "I was more into playing dress-up."

Janice turned her head to the back window where the rabbits had now scattered.

"He used the same shotgun as his father. Passed through generations. I would have been next to have it, but..."

Her delight switched to misery as she moved her attention back to dinner.

"But what?" Faith seemed suddenly hooked on her mum's words.

"It was never found again after...Well." Janice's face crumpled. Absorbed In her thoughts, she couldn't finish the sentence.

"Girls, I think you better go upstairs."

Eric's voice was stern, and it felt unsettling to hear. He gently placed his hand on Janice's back.

"No justice," Janice Mumbled, tears welling in her eyes.

Faith and I stood in unison and hurried out of the kitchen. Her scream echoed up the stairs.

"Still no justice!"

We continued to hear her sob until we reached Faith's room. Faith apologised as she closed her bedroom door.

"She will be okay; Dad will calm her down."

In the way she assured me, I assumed things like that happened a lot. I was at a loss for what to say and felt completely confused by her mum. Faith, I suspected, could read the feelings on my face. Her frustration flared. But something more was weighing over her, and it had been throughout the evening. She hesitated for a moment before speaking.

"I've been thinking the same thought since I met you, Melissa."

She noticed the drop in my expression.

"No, no, nothing bad, I just...I wondered...I." She took a deep sigh.

"I think I figured out another part about me. And it involves you."

My airways felt constricted, and I began to hear every heartbeat.

"I think I like you more than a friend, Mel."

She had planned it all along. She plotted the plan of attack alongside Victoria and Bea, claiming her place as the third friend. They were clever. Revealing my secret when I felt most vulnerable, stretched it out long enough for me to believe Faith cared for me. It was my fault for being so trusting. My fault that I'm faced with another loss because I created false hope.

Chapter Nine
Faith

I felt so humiliated. Melissa made me feel in a way that was so unknown, I assumed it was because I had feelings towards her. All evening I had been sure about what I would say to her. But it felt wrong even before the words left my mouth. It was nothing more than a friendship and the cost of figuring out my confusion wasn't worth it.

She labelled me a liar and ran out, leaving me speechless. I followed her after a few seconds, stunned in silence. But as I reached the middle of the stairs the front door slammed, causing an increase of whimpers from the kitchen. It was Mum. I felt my temper shorten each time she broke. I hated that part of myself. She had no control over what she was going through or how her mind reacted to situations. I knew I had to remain patient as she tried to get better.

As I had expected, she was still sitting at the kitchen table. I presumed to see Dad still consoling her, but she was alone.

"I ruined it again for you, haven't I?" Her soft voice felt fatigued.

I dreaded the fact the front door was visible from the kitchen. If it wasn't, Mum wouldn't assume she was the reason for Melissa's sudden leave when I was the one to blame.

"No, Mum. I did this time." My throat swelled, "we were speaking and... I said the wrong thing."

Mum straightened her curled posture and looked towards me. She pulled the dining chair next to her and patted the seat cushion for me to sit. I rested my head on her chest as I sat down. Her fingers brushed through my hair.

A continental breakfast spread would usually be at the table the morning after Mum's worst days. It was the first thing that sprung to mind as I woke up, signalling how dreadful the day before must have been.

"Faith?"

Mum called my name from downstairs. I wasn't sure how many times she'd called before I eventually woke up. So, I decided to not let myself fall back into sleep and feed the hunger signals that had now begun to grow.

Towards the table's edge was a single plate with a dusting of toast crumbs.

"Is that you, Faith?"

Mum called once again. Her energized voice was in sharp contrast to the night before. Clips from heels approached closer until Mum's happy face came into sight.

"Oh good! I've invited Ethan over since I know you were upset about your friend yesterday. I figured seeing an old friend might help you forget about it."

She had made such a huge judgement without discussing it with me first. She smiled, wanting me to confirm I was okay with it. But there wasn't a reason for Ethan to visit. He wasn't an old friend; he was still a stranger. It was worrying to see Mum revert to wanting my old life to return. I smiled back in response, hoping she did only invite him in hopes of cheering me up. Mum picked up her reflective purse from the dust-covered sideboard.

"And I made the decision to do the same. So today I'm meeting some old friends from where we used to live."

She took out her lip gloss and applied it using her reflection from the purse. It would be my first time home without Mum and I wasn't sure how I would feel without her.

"Is Dad going with you too?"

I noticed I hadn't seen him since dinner.

"He's piled high with work." A concerned line appeared in the middle of her eyebrows, "he is overworked but still insists on being the sole provider in this home."

Dad's reasoning for Mum not to go back to work was understandable. Adding more stress to her already-stressed state could make her worse.

"He's on his way back with Ethan, and they should be here soon."

"Here soon?" I stuttered.

She said it in such a casual way, which I had never seen her do before. I had no idea how many times she had called me, so I buried my anger at her for not waking me up earlier. I needed to hurry up and get ready, but I didn't want to interrupt Mum's cheerful mood by leaving her in the middle of our conversation. She handed me a fifty-pound note and closed it in my hand, oblivious to my response.

"Your father will most likely be at meetings all day and I haven't prepared any dinner, so get something nice for you and Ethan to eat."

She clipped her heels out of the kitchen, giving me the freedom to get ready.

Jogging bottoms and a tank top tempted my eyes as I peered into my closet. I didn't need to impress Ethan but I wondered if Mum would expect me to dress up a bit more. Then, the box next to my closet caught my attention. One of the few boxes still packed with clothes. A neon crop top was the first thing I saw when I opened it previously. Coupled with my tiredness from unpacking, I left the box figuring it held clothes I wouldn't wear anyway. But it had now begun to intrigue me enough to explore the rest of the clothes within it. I reopened the two cardboard squares and removed the semi-sticky tape I re-used to seal it with. But it only reinforced my initial thought. I wondered how I had come to wear the clothing I wasn't reaching for in the past.

The front door was unlatched. Knowing Mum's habit of not letting guests knock, I knew Ethan had arrived. I threw on the jogging bottoms and the tank top that first caught my eye and crept downstairs, wanting to see him before he saw me. He looked different. His trimmed brown hair was shaven and dyed violet. Was it even Ethan? There were no distinguishing features of his I could remember. Ethan's face was plain, his eyes kind, but the hair blurred a clear memory of his appearance. I knew I couldn't stay on the stairs forever, no matter how torn my mind was. I stepped into the kitchen like I hadn't seen him come in. This wasn't new to Mum since she tended to open the front door unannounced.

"Faith!"

74

Ethan's words interjected the conversation between him and Mum.

"I like your new hair." It was the only response I could think to say to his quick reaction to me.

"It's not new now; I've had it for a while. I haven't seen you in so long!"

I thought I'd never see him again.

"I think we should make our way," Dad quietly said to Mum, not wanting to interrupt our conversation.

"Your dad's driving me to the train station, then is off to his work meetings. If you need anything, use Ethan's mobile," Mum confirmed.

Her words reminded me of the irritation of not allowing me to have my own phone.

"Bye!"

We shouted together as the door closed. I had no idea when either of them would return or how long Ethan would stay.

My hunger signals had continued to increase. I opened the closest wall cabinet; unsure what food Mum had allocated for the day's breakfast. She would usually have everything measured and ready for me before I woke up.

"What are you looking for?"

Ethan had almost slipped my mind.

"Breakfast." I reacted as if I hadn't forgotten about him.

"Thank God, I didn't have a chance to eat before your father came and got me!"

I couldn't bear the mental anguish of worrying if the measurement error in Mum's food would set her off. If it was only me, it could have been okay. As he responded I closed the cupboard, unsure how I would make it 'til dinner.

"If there's nothing there, we could go somewhere to eat breakfast?"

My dissatisfaction seeped through to my face.

"Or I could get something for us and bring it back?" He swiftly followed up.

He started rummaging through his pockets, clinking coins as he did. The muscles in my face loosened. He was willing to pay. It was difficult to understand, but they all lost someone they adored. And I was that someone. I started to feel awful about not putting in more effort with Ethan.

"Mum gave me money for us to use for food. Spend half on our breakfast, and we'll use the other half for lunch."

He slipped his hands out of his pockets and took the fifty-pound note from my grip.

"I would come with you, but Mum doesn't like the house empty."

I wasn't sure whether it was true and it would almost certainly come back to haunt me, but him knowing the truth would make someone else feel unwelcome in the house. He turned away with a false smile, one Mum often did. And I knew he didn't believe what I said.

I walked upstairs as soon as he left. Staying in the kitchen had begun reminding me of the previous evening, and I spent the morning trying to keep it out. Mum's cry was still echoing in my head, and I couldn't help to wonder what it meant. No justice? I tried to remember the conversation that was happening beforehand. Something stirred Mum. Granddad's gun. As soon as Dad told us to go upstairs, I forgot she mentioned it. I assumed he committed suicide, and they didn't tell Mum because she couldn't handle the reality. Still nothing was clear about Granddad. The cluttered words written behind the photo of the gun jumped to the front of my memory. What letter was it talking about? And who was the one who found it? I knew I had to return to the attic now that I was alone at home.

The pole to get into the attic was wedged beneath the curled carpet on the landing. We were finally making progress with unpacking, so it had to be something that opened the way for the house to appear more orderly. I latched the pole onto the hook and the ladder extended to the floor. The boxes piled higher than last time. I narrowed my eyes and peered around for the labelled boxes I needed. To avoid feeling discouraged, I pulled myself onto the attic floor. The mahogany display cabinet no longer stood out among it all. It seemed they tucked it towards the back of the attic to make room for more boxes. A corner of a box was sticking out from behind the cabinet. It had a label, but I knew I had to get closer to understand what it said. Making my way over felt more complicated than the first time I was up there. But as the letters cleared to read *'family photographs,'* I quickly forgot the effort it took.

"Found it," I whispered to myself.

There was a sudden slamming knock on the front door. I feared it to be Dad, so I grabbed the box. Hidden beneath was the box of Ted's love letters. Trusting my instincts, I also grabbed that one and dashed out of the attic. The pole assisted me in pushing the ladder back in and closing the door behind. Then I raced to my room to bury the boxes beneath my blankets. There was another slamming knock at the door. Surely Dad would have used his keys by now? Blurred violet greeted me as I neared the front door. Ethan had once again slipped my mind. He took so long to bring breakfast that I was now no longer hungry.

"Sorry I was gone so long; the fifty-pound note you gave was a fake one," he said, breathless as he walked through the door.

I was afraid that he thought I had given it to him on purpose.

"Mum gave it to me this morning; I had no idea. I'll tell her to give you back what you spent."

"Don't be silly!"

His response seemed sincere, so I took a seat as he placed a packet of bacon and a dozen eggs on the table.

"Not quite a full English, I know." Ethan laughed and I smiled.

It felt impossible to have empty conversations with Ethan when Mum's cries still lingered in my mind.

"What were you up to while I was gone?" He questioned as he turned on the gas to light the hob.

Would Ethan know about Granddad?

"Looking for the pictures of my granddad."

As I responded, I was aware of his reaction. I couldn't tell if it was a coincidence that he repositioned himself as I said it. Because he hadn't replied back right away, I decided to add more.

"I have no idea how he died," I continued; my gaze still fixed on his reply.

He halted before cracking the egg onto the frying pan, his face in shock.

"You still haven't heard about your grandfather's murder?"

Chapter Ten
Melissa

I had nothing left to lose. Victoria and Bea weren't going to get away with it this time. I grabbed my phone and typed Victoria's name into my contacts. As I scrolled down, I spotted the date and time of her last missed call. The evening I found out Sam was leaving. He never replied to the voicemail I left him; no phone call, no message. I presumed he rethought his forgiveness towards me. My natural state was loneliness at this point, so it almost put me at ease. I snapped myself out of my drifting thoughts and dialled Victoria's number.

"Hello?"

Victoria's voice wasn't as sharp as I had anticipated. Perhaps she didn't recognise me because she had removed my number from her phone, or maybe it was my body reassuring me that this was the right thing for me to do.

"You're a coward for getting Faith to perform your dirty work for you."

Faith was also in the wrong, but I was lenient since I had experienced Victoria's manipulation first-hand.

"I don't use anyone to do my dirty work, especially not a weirdo like Faith."

Her voice became more confrontational. I stood firm in my replies, confident she wouldn't trick me anymore.

"You revealed my secret to her and forced her to wait until I trusted her enough to ruin me."

Her confrontational tone lightened.

"I don't need Faith to ruin you. I did that all by myself."

I could sense her proud smirk at the other end of the phone.

"Faith was one of the only people it didn't get to; Gabriella must have made sure of it."

Gabriella was the first person to console me when it began. I almost didn't want to hear her words align with the truth.

"But now you've reminded me, I'll tell her as soon as I see her next. Nice chat Mel."

I stumbled onto the sofa behind me as she hung up the phone. Faith was sincere. I put her in the same situation that Victoria and Bea did for me. Victoria took pride in her ability to terrorise people; she would never lie about something like that.

Louise was still at the park with Macy and Maddie, and I desperately needed her comforting words. She spent the morning persuading me to go with them, but my head was still swollen with grief.

I decided the way to rest my aching mind was by lying down on my bed. As I walked through the landing, hazy violet crept closer to the front door. Then a face pressed the door's glass, jolting me to the wall. Was I about to get burgled? They weren't a brilliant thief with hair so identifiable. Two knocks followed. I'd seen enough horror films to know not to open it.

"Melissa, it's me, Faith."

Faith? How did she always seem to appear when I needed her most? I couldn't figure out who the other person would be with her.

"Please, Melissa, open the door; I have just learned something unbelievable."

Maybe Victoria had already got to her. But I didn't feel the same fear I used to. So I made the decision to open the door.

The hazy violet cleared to a shortly-shaven head. He took a step forward, his smile uncomfortable. Faith also took a step forward, putting herself in front of him.

"This is Ethan. He's..."

She took a breath and stopped before continuing.

"An old friend."

His gaze moved to the ground. Faith kept on with her hurried words, still not mentioning our fallout.

"He just told me about Shotgun."

Hearing that name dazed me. It was no longer spoken. Of Course, we were all like Faith when we were first aware it happened. It was all the town spoke of, and it's what our community became known for. It caused such havoc that the majority of the residents left. Those that stayed became too afraid to speak about it, so they pretended it never happened to return to their everyday lives. There was a string of unsolved attacks and robberies before the murder, with only one recorded sighting of him. Rumour had it that it came from the person he had killed and that it was the reason for his death. Shortly after they made their statement, they retracted it. But the fact the killer had a shotgun had already gotten to the public. Upon discovering that the bullet that killed the victim came from the same gun, they gave him the name Shotgun.

It *was* unbelievable, but I was unsure why she brought her new knowledge to me. Maybe she assumed I wasn't aware of it? But, on the contrary, I was more surprised this was the first she heard about the unsolved murder case; it had gone so far outside of town.

I accidentally returned a blank stare. I couldn't decide whether my first words to Faith should be an apology for leaving her house in such a state, or how the entire country already knew about the murder.

"It was awful when it all happened. The victim's family never got closure."

I toned down my answer, not wanting to mention that the entire community stayed terrified that he would attack again. There was a sudden worry that Faith would follow the people out of the town. Ethan turned his head to me as an immediate reaction after I spoke.

"The victim was Faith's grandfather."

Faith clutched her chest and screamed in pain as she collapsed down. Ethan dropped down to her eye level and shouted in a panic.

"Should I call an ambulance? What's wrong?"

"No, I'm okay now."

Fear and confusion had paralysed me. This wasn't something I had seen Faith experience, yet it felt disturbingly recognisable to me. I needed to ensure she was okay, so I extended one arm to her, Ethan took the other, and we helped her inside. As we reached the living room, she untangled her arms from ours and promised us that she didn't need our attention.

"But back to what I was saying."

She continued speaking as if nothing had happened.

"They still have not found my granddad's murderer, and I think I might have some unknown evidence."

The fact that Ted White was Faith's granddad still hadn't sunk in. How was I just aware of that fact when I had known Faith a while?

"How do you know its evidence?" I asked.

She reached into her pocket and pulled out a folded photograph. As she unfolded the edges, it showed a gun sat within a display cabinet. My eyes widened.

"This was his gun that went missing, maybe even before the burglaries began to happen."

They shot him with his own gun? She turned over the photo and my eyes followed the words written on the back.

"He found my letter, run as far away as possible," I read quietly aloud.

"Why are you showing me this? You need to show this to the police!" I immediately added.

Faith retracted the photo as she backtracked on her words.

"They searched his house when he died, and they must have not found a strong link to take it as evidence."

Or they might not have found it, I thought.

"And I'm showing it to you because it's an unsolved case."

She stared at me as if she expected me to understand what she meant by those words.

"Our school project?" She added.

"No way."

I threw up my hands and backed out of the room. If Faith was going to use her grandfather's death for a school project, I wanted no part in it. She followed me into the kitchen.

"I have more of his things at my house; we could find a lead that wasn't even thought of by the police."

I cut her off in the middle of her rambling.

"Shotgun could be living in this town for all we know; he was never identified. This is not the type of thing to use for a school project, Faith; it can put us in serious danger."

We would be the next victims if it was confirmed that her granddad's murder was due to him knowing something. No potential high grades were worth dying for.

"It's for more than the school project." She locked her gaze on mine, "my granddad deserves justice."

Faith's mum's cry became a whirlwind in my mind. The catastrophe wreaked havoc on the town, but it hit her family harder. It had broken her mum. Faith appeared to have given up attempting to heal her, which may have made her feel that doing this would help her mum recover. She didn't grasp how unlikely it was that we'd find anything more than the police had, let alone solve the crime. But I felt ready to follow her hope.

"Fine," I exhaled.

She grinned and reached in for a hug. Her voice became vibrant.

"I'll bring what I've got in on Monday."

Ethan strolled into the kitchen as he heard her tone alter. He put one arm around her and pulled her closer for a kiss on the cheek. Faith dodged it by ducking under his arm and made her way to the front door.

"See you Monday!" I replied as Ethan trailed behind her.

What she discovered seemed to overpower her memory of how I reacted when she asked to date me. I felt relieved, although left confused by the situation. I never saw her feelings reciprocated by how she acted around me. She had no idea if I even liked girls but was bold enough to ask. Even though I knew so much about Faith's life, most still remained a mystery to me.

It began to dawn on me what it was that I had agreed to. And it wasn't the school project that I felt frightened by. The whispers and rumours were still stopping me from returning to school. Victoria and Bea had a firm grasp on my future at Dawnton, and I knew there was only one way to break away from them.

I restarted my disrupted journey to my bedroom and sat at my computer. Sweat beaded on my forehead as the keyboard glued to my fingertips with each letter I typed. I was about to update my status with the two words that drowned my thoughts since I was young. Two words that caused so much self-hatred that I projected on to others. Two words that were going to give me back control. Two words that I finally accepted were true. Two words to be free.

'I'm gay.'

Chapter Eleven
Faith

I hated the unsettling feeling of going into an empty schoolyard in the middle of the day. The frantic crowds of the first bell, when I had English as my first lesson, felt a lot better than entering on my own.

I counted the minutes until it was time to leave the house for school. Initially, Dad's focus would be on education at home. He had the times for each lesson planned out and taught me strictly to the school's curriculum. His dislike of English was probably why it was the lesson he chose for me to learn in school. I didn't inherit his hatred. English gave me the fulfilment I hadn't experienced in any other class. Mrs Beckett confirmed it when she said she could see my love of writing in every piece of work I produced. It was either the stress with Mum or his ever-increasing workload that caused my schooling to fade. That day, I was grateful for the lack of home-schooling. I needed to shift their concentration away as I moved Granddad's photos and letters out of the house. I questioned if I should have accepted Ethan's offer to help grab more of his belongings but feared I would have lost it all if we got caught.

Students still repelled away from Melissa. Victoria grabbed my arm as I walked into class before Melissa noticed I was there.

"Did you see what Mel updated her status as at the weekend?" She smirked.

Not having a phone made me miss yet another thing.

"No?" I said, provoking her reply.

She peered over to check if Mrs Beckett was looking, then took her phone from her pocket and pointed the screen towards me.

"She's gay?" I whispered.

Perhaps what I revealed forced her to confront her sexuality.

"Apparently, she only wrote that to cover up that she wanted to date her brother."

Bea's gag was loud enough to draw Melissa's attention to us. Melissa's face grew with worry, triggering Gabriella's words to resurface in my memory.

"You talk so much shit, Victoria."

I raised my voice enough for Melissa to hear. Victoria backed away, and I left her fumbling on her reply. I lifted the boxes I had placed on the ground and walked to Melissa.

"Are you alright?" I asked as I sat on the chair beside her.

"I'm sorry for how I left your house the other day." Melissa's face flushed with shame. Her bringing it up surprised me. Perhaps her reaction *was* due to her own sexuality.

"Don't mention it." I reacted nonchalantly, "I've had problems identifying my feelings since the coma." I placed both boxes on the table in front of us, "it was exactly what I needed to realise that my feelings for you were friendship."

I felt relieved that everything was finally clear. Melissa's expression softened.

"What is that?"

She drew her eyes to the boxes.

"Family photos and love letters Ted wrote to his wife."

She returned my stare, unconvinced.

"It will help us build an image around who he was," I reassured her.

I drew the family photographs box closer to me and took a stack of photos out. Then, one by one, I placed them on the table.

Melissa chuckled to herself.

"How many bad pictures were there of you that you took out before?"

If she believed I'd be in the photos, it proved I wasn't over-thinking it. It felt easier to lie to avoid any unanswerable questions she would follow it up with. But this whole case was going to be uncomfortable, and I knew I wouldn't be able to ignore it all the time.

"None." I was quick in my reply.

She laughed again. "Yeah, right."

I stayed silent in her disbelief. It wasn't my fault she didn't believe what I said.

"So, girls?"

Mrs Beckett's voice startled us both.

"What was your deciding project idea?"

She extended her neck and narrowed her eyes to the laid-out photos.

"Persuading we've solved unsolvable crimes."

As I stated it, she seemed to recognise my granddad in the photos. She took a step back and gulped as she briefly closed her eyes.

"Faith, I know this is such a difficult and terrible time for you and your family, but this isn't what you should be doing." Her sympathetic voice sounded laced with fear.

Mrs Becket was the biggest roadblock in beginning the project, which I had never considered. She was the one who chose the topic and was in charge of marking the end piece, so she had complete control. I started racking my brain for a way to persuade her.

"But it's too late to start brainstorming other ideas."

I assumed Melissa would also try and convince Mrs Beckett, but she remained quiet.

"It would be irresponsible of me to let this happen, sorry Faith."

My strategy wasn't going to work. It would have been easier to agree and come up with another idea, but something was urging me to pursue this one. So, I had no choice but to manipulate my persuasiveness.

"It's the only thing that helps me get through the grief process."

Her brows dipped in sympathy.

"His death has consumed all my thoughts. Doing this is allowing me to finally process it."

It felt awful to tell Mrs Beckett such a manipulative lie, but I knew it was necessary.

"I don't want to be the one to get in the way of you dealing with such a difficult situation, but this isn't acceptable for a school project, Faith."

Her words began to sound like Melissa's initial reaction. I started to feel hopeless. Then, Melissa's glare at me caught my eye. She returned her attention to Mrs Beckett.

"You, me and Faith will be the only ones who know we're doing it. We're not going to let it spread around the class. Especially now that things are starting to feel more normal." Melissa lowered her gaze to the photographs, "I wouldn't want to put that fear back into anyone."

"Well," Mrs Beckett exhaled. "Only if you're sure."

I hid the picture of his gun in my jean pocket at home. It seemed far too important to leave it out in the open at school. The aim was to figure out who Granddad was as a person. At first, I was hesitant to trust Mum's naturally biased descriptions of him. Still, they matched the joy shown in the photographs. Ted seemed to be a good man who didn't deserve to die like he did. Although I didn't know him, he was the only person in my family I felt a connection to. I averted my tear-filled gaze from Melissa as she returned to the table with a large sheet of paper. We spent the lesson building more of a back narrative for him and by the end, the piece of paper was completely full.

"We will have to start on the letters next lesson," I suggested.

"You're so lucky you get to go home now," Melissa replied as she folded the large piece of paper to be more compact.

It didn't feel like luck when I got home. Mum stood at my bedroom door, etched with a familiar expression. Something had to have provoked her again. But, of course, I got the boxes tucked under my blankets before she realised I was home. So it couldn't have been that unless she noticed they were missing from the attic. I dreaded the words she was about to speak.

"It was so nice to see my old friends again."

The tension in my chest was released. We hadn't had a chance to catch up about her time away. She stayed overnight with her friends, and I was already asleep before she arrived home.

"It gave me the feeling of returning to who I was before everything happened."

I smiled, sensing that she had more to say.

"So, me and your father." She mentioned Dad like a second thought. "We booked a hotel back where we lived, just for a little bit."

What she was saying didn't make any sense to me. "A hotel for what?"

My expression reflected my puzzled thoughts.

"We're all moving back for a while."

My life was about to alter drastically just as things were beginning to work out. There was more to know about Granddad, and doing it while away from his home would be tough. How was I to tell Melissa? My search had to continue for Granddad's killer, and I couldn't do it in a shared hotel room with Mum and Dad. She would have to search through his handwritten letters on her own. Mum was still at my door, waiting for me to respond. I wanted to scream. But I needed her to disappear to give Melissa the box in secret. So, I put on a façade.

"That's fine," I answered. "But can I say goodbye to Melissa before we leave?"

My acceptance of it shocked her.

"Of course, but don't be too long!"

She walked away from my door frame and out of sight. I yanked the blankets from the boxes and grabbed the box I needed to give her.

I felt grateful Melissa had written down her address because I needed to reach her so many times and couldn't without a phone. Her house was not at all like mine. It wasn't the size difference that struck me; first, it was the sensation. I felt at ease there. Mine was still only a house, but hers felt more like a home to me. Melissa's aunt gave a cheerful grin as she opened the door.

"Hello, Faith; I'm afraid Mel is still at school!" She turned her head over to the clock on the wall and then at her watch. "She won't be back for a while yet."

I thought leaving it with her aunt would be more straightforward than facing Melissa.

"Could you hand it over to her? It's for a project at school."

She lifted the box from my fingers and glanced into my eyes.

"I appreciate you helping her get back into school." Her tone was soft, "if it hadn't been for you, I don't think she would have ever gone back."

Guilt quivered at the corner of my smile.

Chapter Twelve
Melissa

F aith's granddad's letters had a sticky note attached to the top of the pile.

'I have to move back to my old town for a while. See what you can find.'

My eyes felt wounded as I read the words. My mind flashed to the moment I discovered Sam was leaving. Once again, I was their second thought. Both never said anything to my face. No reason why or when she would return. I put the box of letters to the side and ignored my thoughts as I walked back downstairs. I noticed the steam from the spaghetti cooking on the stove had made the kitchen windows blur. Louise had a habit of forgetting to open the window before starting to cook. She's the only one to ever set off the smoke alarm. We'd be in fits of laughter, leaping to switch it off amid the piercing sound and wondering what cursed our family for having such short genes.

"School project not going well?"

Louise was always aware of my emotions, no matter how well I thought I could cover them. I knew I couldn't act as if nothing was wrong because my feelings were clearly already visible on my face. Sam shared my thoughts with Faith. It felt easier to bring him up to Louise.

"No, Sam hasn't responded to the voicemail I left him."

She slid a wooden spoon into the Bolognese and began stirring it.

"Try calling him again; there might be a good reason why he hasn't."

The only reason that ever sprung to mind was the long flight over made him reflect on everything I had done, making him vow never to speak to me again.

"Don't be too long, though; dinners almost ready," she added.

"I'll probably only be a second," I muttered.

In the slim chance he would answer, I chose to go back into my room to call him, away from Macy's, Maddie's and even Louise's hearing.

Every second that followed each ring made me worry it would go to voicemail again. Until I heard an answer.

"Oh God, Mel, I completely forgot to get back to ya!"

That was all? My brain couldn't fathom the fact that all he did was forget.

"I thought you didn't want to speak to me."

I replied playfully. It was the only way I could think to tell the truth but avoid confrontation.

"Oh, Mel I'm so sorry. It's been so hectic. We lost our luggage and had problems with the house we were moving into. The weather 'as been great 'ere, though."

My head turned to my open window. Raindrops had fallen onto the window seal after I neglected to close it before school, "the weather is not great here."

Sam giggled, "nothing's changed then?"

There was so much bottled-up anger in my chest that it began to hurt. I thought I would feel a release after Sam answered the phone. But it was all still there.

"Apart from you leaving me."

Stillness grew. But I didn't regret voicing my hurt.

"Mel."

His voice started to crack. But I found it difficult to empathise with him when my feelings were clearly unimportant.

"It was too trauma'ic for Mum to go back to work or find a new job in town. She tried, but she couldn't, not after what 'ad 'appened. She needed a new start."

It was the most significant attack Shotgun had done at the time. It was the morning, and the bank was empty after the rush of the elderly getting their pensions. Apart from Sam's mum, who was at work that day, and Ted White, who, according to Sam's mum, was rushing to cash a check he had forgotten about. A man in a balaclava yelled as he came up behind Sam's mum. He told her to give him money, forcing her by holding the shotgun to her head. A sudden thought ignited in my brain. Ted must have recognised the gun as his own.

"I wish I could have told you, but I didn't know how. By the time Mum said we were moving; it was too late."

I felt terrible convincing myself to believe he had a choice in moving so far away.

"Dinner!" Louise called from downstairs.

"I know, Sam. It was all just so confusing. I've missed you so much."

"I've missed you too. And I'm only a phone call away if you need anything, and I'll remember to answer this time."

We both chuckled and said our goodbyes, which seemed to fill the void he left by not saying goodbye to me before.

Louise appeared at my door holding a tray with a plate of Bolognese as I hung up the phone.

"I didn't know if you preferred to eat up here today."

As she left the tray on my bed, I thanked her. But I didn't feel that hungry anymore. The tray was next to the box of Faith's granddad's letters. I had attempted to ignore them because it triggered the familiar feeling of abandonment. But, like with Sam, was I over-thinking it? I returned my attention to the words on the sticky note. She shouldn't be away for long if she wanted me to continue rummaging through his belongings. The case, at one point, overtook everyone's life and I was letting untouched letters that could hold information sit there out of stubbornness. I brought the box to my lap and removed the top letter to read. Dirt had stained the paper and the handwriting made it challenging to begin.

'Please accept my apologies for not responding to you as quickly as you responded to me. I've never met someone quite like you.'

My eyes examined the following few sentences but I couldn't make out anything more. I picked up the next letter and it mirrored the challenging handwriting as before. Was that all it was going to be? I took out the entire stack, flipping over each one to see if my brain could grasp any of the written words. Each was revealed to be the same and I began to question whether it was worth continuing. I made a mental note of which part of the pile I'd stop looking at; it didn't feel right to give up searching so soon. So I flipped through the rest, only seeing single words that were clear to read.

The first distinguishable letter came to sight when the pile neared the centre. The colour of the ink had altered and the words were larger, making it more readable. Ted continued to address it to Betty. He kept writing letters to her as if she could still read them, even though it was clear she had died. He wrote the next letters the same. But then

I notice a change in his writing style. He continued to address the letters to Betty, but it began to feel more like a diary than letters to her. It shifted from him expressing his longing for her and reminiscing old memories to his concerns and aspirations for the future. It seemed like a positive shift, and I wondered if it was a new method for him to deal with her passing.

I read through the letters for hours and began recognising the intricacies of the town events he described. I assumed the lack of mention of Faith was because he wrote them before her birth, but now that seemed impossible. The pile of letters lessened, and the date drew nearer to the present. It was unsettling to see him write about earlier attacks while knowing that the same attacker would take his life. I peered at the date of the letter to see if my memory matched. The armed bank robbery was next. I lifted the letter to unveil it, but there were only a few words on the page.

'So, I had to retract my statement. God only knows what he can do to her; it'd be my fault. She needs to know immediately.

All my love
Ted'

The end of a letter. The writing on the back of the photo resurfaced in my mind. Was this the letter it was referring to? The first page must have contained something that put him in danger. The hair on my body stood on end. Shotgun must have taken the letter.

I was at a loss for what to do. The first page would have long since vanished, so it had no purpose other than to explain why he had pulled his statement. What more did he see in the bank robbery? The hours spent reading the letters felt like a waste. Nothing got me any closer to

97

figuring out who was responsible for his death. I gathered all the letters into a bundle and carried them over to the box. As I was about to place them in, I noticed the corner fold at the bottom of the box had risen. I placed the letters down beside me and lifted the bottom corner. Between the cardboard that created the flap, two folded pieces of paper were wedged. The first I opened was short letter, but this time addressed to Janice. It was the same handwriting that was on the back of the photograph.

'Janice, his name is Roman Woodson.'

As I read what was on the second folded paper, my knees dropped to the floor.

Chapter Thirteen
Faith

Mum adopted a cheery demeanour as we drove away from Dawnton, which she maintained throughout the ride back to our old town. As we moved closer to the old house, it surprised me that I could still recognise the streets. But as a result, I was aware as Dad took a detour to avoid driving past it. I imagined he didn't want to ruin Mum's mood by the concrete drive.

"Here it is!"

We took a slow drive up a road to a set of scaffolded buildings.

"Are you sure?" Mum responded with concern.

Dad made the arrangement of the hotel without Mum. He was hesitant to let her arrange anything else after what happened with the painters and decorators when we first moved into Granddad's house.

"The entrance is at the back," he assured her.

It was a long climb up the stairs, and I couldn't understand why Dad had chosen this hotel for us to stay in. It didn't even appear to be a finished build. Dad became ecstatic as he hopped up the last few stairs to the front of what appeared to be our hotel room.

"I'll be your tour guide."

Dad exaggerated the pronunciation of his words. He spotted the disappointment on Mum's face that had grown as we walked up the stairs and, I suspected, tried to restore her smile.

Futuristic lines greeted us as he brought us into the room. The further I walked in, the more I felt disheartened to discover a single bed behind the wall. The only thing visible from the door was a double bed, so there was a hope that I would have a room separate from them. A computer rested on a sleek white desk at the head of my bed. As soon as I discovered it, I audibly gasped. Perhaps staying in our old town wouldn't be so bad after all.

I entered the on-suite, where Dad was still showing Mum around and I pretended I didn't notice the computer to avoid ruining my chances of going on it.

"Did you like the room, Faith?" Dad asked, pleased with himself.

"Let me have a look." Mum spoke first before I was able to respond to Dad. Then, she exited the on-suite and went to the wall lamps that overlooked the double bed, "we used to have these in our old bedroom, didn't we, Eric?"

"I thought you would have noticed them." Dad sounded delighted that she did.

She sat on the bed, her gaze fixed on the back wall's window. Dad came up and wrapped his arm around her, "I'm excited about our date later."

She pressed her head to his shoulder.

I didn't ask questions about their date since I assumed something would trigger Mum before they left, but they were out the door before it darkened. It was becoming clear how different Mum had been since returning, but it made me wonder why they didn't tell me their plans.

My confusion didn't linger long, though. As soon as Mum and Dad went, I dashed to the computer. I didn't expect to be able to get on it so quickly. My brain began to flush out questions that had taken over my mind, knowing that I now had something that could finally help me solve them. Thoughts of Melissa repeated themselves over. Energy ignited between us each time we were near, which now I knew was not a desire to be in a relationship with her. I needed to know what it was. What to type emerged in my thoughts.

'Unexplainable strong connection with a stranger.'

The connection began the moment I laid eyes on her. Something compelled me to join her group on my first day at Dawnton. My eyes scanned the results that reflected off the screen.

'...If the connection feels spiritual, it could be a sign that God deliberately placed them there.'

I exited the page after registering that I had entered a religious blog by accident. I already had enough uncertainty in my thoughts without adding the possibility of a higher power being in charge of it all. But the idea of a God jogged my mind to one of the project concepts I'd overheard in class. Life after death. A sudden agony pierced my chest once again. It was getting more frequent. The pain had been so intense that I couldn't figure out where it was coming from in my chest. But this time, I was confident. It was from my heart. I did my best to refocus my attention on the computer by not allowing it to consume my thoughts. It was how I always dealt with it. But it was becoming difficult to ignore.

'What happens to your soul after you die?'

My fingers felt compelled to type the words. My eyes scanned through the paragraphs of endless links. I knew I had to continue pushing until I found what I was looking for.

'Sharing the same soul.'

My gaze momentarily slowed as I read the subheading. It held my focus.

'They say you can only share the same soul if you're in a parallel reality. So, if you think you are, you might be right. But keep in mind that everything happens for a purpose. There's a reason you've come this far.'

My eyelids slid open, allowing a flood of light to pass through. Smoke obscured my vision. The light from the lamppost shone from the bricks on either side of me; I was in a back alley. A shadow of a figure approached. Something cleared in my vision. A gun. Granddad's shotgun. I lowered my head to see where it was aiming. My heart. But as I looked down, I realised it wasn't my hair. It looked more like... Melissa's?

A knock on the hotel door startled me. I shut down the computer and rushed to open the door in case it was Mum and Dad returning early from their date. As I was about to turn the doorknob, I took a deep breath and reminded myself that it was probably room service. A girl stood at eye level with me. Her dark curls, unfastened from her ponytail, twirled in her fingers.

"Faith?"

She recognised me. It left me unable to speak.

"Of course, you have no idea who I am anymore."

She allowed herself into the hotel room.

"Your mum messaged me." She shifted her gaze to the side, "well, she tried Ethan first, but he was out of town." She picked up the complimentary biscuits left on the counter, "anyway, she was nervous about leaving you here alone, so she asked me to come by."

She took a self-tour of the room.

"I'm Jasmine, by the way."

Her name provoked no recognition. I didn't know where to begin when it came to responding to her. She seemed to have handled the news of my memory loss much better than Ethan had, so there wasn't a worry about upsetting her with direct questions.

"How did I know you?" I asked.

She switched her focus back to me and leaned against the wall. She struggled, rummaging through her pocket, "I actually brought pictures from my birthday party."

She handed over a pile of crumpled Polaroid photos. I stacked them behind each other, immediately noticing the alcohol bottles in each photo. In the pictures we took together, not one had my face in focus.

"It was the last time I saw you." She lowered her sight to the photos in my hands, "we were pretty close."

The presence of alcohol made me curious, "is that where it happened?

She raised her eyes to me. "Wow, you still don't know?"

Her reaction was understandable, yet it still surprised me. With a shake of my head, I replied, "I don't think about it too much."

"Maybe you should."

There wasn't a desire to learn how I ended up in a coma in the first place anymore. I often wondered if I would be more concerned if I wasn't so cut off from my previous life. I knew that if I figured out what had put me there, it wouldn't affect the impact of whatever it was that had happened to my brain. It became distressing if I thought about it too much, so it stayed shut in my mind.

"So, you know nothing about your life before?" Her voice tinged with excitement.

"Mum's told me stories, but I suppose it's difficult to keep memories of people that are not part of your already established memory."

She nodded as though she understood, "I used to not know anyone on my mum's side of the family, but I used that website to do the finding out for me."

She laughed for a moment before pausing, "maybe you should check out that website?"

I wasn't sure if she expected me to know the website she was referring to. But learning more about family members I didn't know wasn't at the top of my list of priorities. Although, in the silence that followed, I realised that becoming more conscious of the family members in Mum's stories could bring Mum so much happiness. I got Jasmine to the computer and let her type it into the search bar.

"Okay, since you are an only child, your known family tree starts with you," Jasmine said.

I sat on my pillow and watched her type my full name, birth year, and current address into the information box. She was more confident in her knowledge of me than I was. She let out a puzzled grunt as she refreshed the page and re-wrote my information for the third time.

"That's weird; it doesn't recognise any of your information." She sat motionlessly; her puzzled stare fixed on the computer screen, "oh well, we can begin with your mum."

She regained her previous energy level and knew just what to type into the computer for Mum. Once she finished typing, cartoon tree branches grew from mum's name.

"See, look, it shows her direct relatives."

Her siblings emerged from the branches. Under their names were their dates of birth and if and how they died. But their names must not have been retained in my head from Mum's stories because they read foreign to my brain.

"Edward White and Elizabeth White," I read aloud.

The branches to her parents were the only names I recognised.

"Ethan told me that he couldn't understand why no one told you about how he died," she said, slanting her eyebrows at me. "How are you handling it now that he's told you?"

I didn't feel compelled to lie about how I felt about Granddad as I did with other family members. He was the first person who was in my life before the coma that I felt a connection with.

"It was a shock as he told me, but it brought a lot of things together to make sense."

It didn't feel appropriate to mention I was attempting to figure out who killed him. Jasmine returned her attention back to the computer with a sympathetic half-smile.

All evening I attempted to calm the anxiety of Mum and Dad returning. However, I flinched each time I heard a slight noise outside the hotel door; this time, Jasmine noticed.

"Are you okay?"

With a slight bit of embarrassment, I replied, "Mum and Dad will likely return soon, and I don't think they want me to be on the computer."

She appeared to understand it quite quickly. She swung around the corner to view the hotel door before returning her gaze back to the computer.

"Then we will have to be quick," she replied.

105

I interrupted her typing as I saw her write in Dad's first name on the branch, "it's pointless to fill in my dad's information."

She took a break from her typing.

"No there is. I'll try to discover your dad's side more before they return home. Rather than only focusing on your mum." She tried to reassure me, but she misunderstood.

"Dad was an orphan."

She gave me a look of confusion, "this is perfect then; he can learn more about his family."

She continued to write the rest of Dad's name, "it's worth a try."

The same message popped up on screen when she typed in his information as when she typed in mine. He didn't match anyone on any of the records. I assumed because Dad was an orphan, it would prevent certain documents from reaching the internet. I watched her repeatedly refreshing the website, altering single letters and digits each time.

"I can't tell what I filled in wrong," she sighed. "I'll have to do it the long way."

As she clicked on Mum's name, a personal profile appeared. She hovered her mouse over marriages and scrolled down. There was still no mention of Dad. Finally, after watching flashes of web pages Jasmine clicked through, a branch emerged from Mum's name. But it didn't read as Eric Matthews. Instead, the name that appeared on the screen was Roman Woodson.

Chapter Fourteen
Melissa

*J*anice,
     I am writing multiple letters so if he takes them, there will be others. I left written notes on the back of items he wouldn't expect and I hope to God they find their way to you. I'm sending this one through the mail and getting my dear friend Elsie to write the address, so if you didn't recognise the handwriting on the front, it was intentional.

Eric isn't who he claims to be. You must leave him, go as far away as possible, and whatever you do, do not inform him of this letter.

He claimed that a build-up of wildlife nests was interfering with his new business endeavour and asked for my shotgun to be rid of the problem. I thought it odd because nature has never taken over your house before. Since I use my gun frequently, as you know, I wasn't sure if going without it for a few days would result in any issues. I gave him alternative extinction strategies and even suggested shotgun dealers. He insisted, though, that he required mine. Despite my uncertainty, I allowed him to borrow the gun. But only for a short while. I became irate when weeks passed, and he still had not given it back. My attempts to call him ended in voicemail. I considered getting in touch with you, but that discussion about keeping your and Eric's professional lives apart kept running through my thoughts. I was aware that was what kept your marriage together. I didn't want to start a fight between you or bring you any discomfort, Janice. But now I've done just that because I remained silent. I'm sorry; it's all my fault. I'm hoping one day you'll be able to forgive me.

I told myself that if he didn't return it by the end of the month, I would say to you anyway.

I neglected to cash the cheque I had received from Elsie for my birthday throughout the weeks of worry and uncertainty regarding my gun. Because I intended to use the money to travel up north, she had been nagging me to do it. I grabbed the cheque and hurried to the post office as soon as the notion entered my head; I was determined not to lose the thought again. It was then when it happened. Eric was the one who committed the bank robbery, Janice. He was wearing a balaclava, but I saw him holding my gun. I didn't want any harm to come to you, so I retracted my statement from the police and stayed silent. I had to take the matter into my own hands. When I knew you were both out, I used the spare key you gave me to get into your house. I had no choice; I had to find my gun before he did more harm. And it was then that I discovered his records. In his office, tucked away. Roman Woodson is his real name, and he has ties to powerful and violent groups. The entire Woodson line has. The name was recognisable to me because it was the same as his father's. Their family line is notorious for its drug networks. When I was young, a sizable drug raid made headlines worldwide. It stayed prevalent in my head because it was a few miles from the centre of town, working in the surrounding countryside of Dawnton. After all these years, I still remember the name. The Woodsons are extremely dangerous and manipulative. Eric even had me fooled. Someone old enough to remember his grandfather's famous arrest. Eric's father escaped and became a fugitive for many years. He was at one time Britain's most wanted man. Roman Woodson. His name was everywhere. Every paper had his face. It wasn't a face that drew similar to your husband's; otherwise, I would have known who he was. Eventually, they found him with a changed identity, living a regular life. He had a child, one son, Roman Woodson jr. Lived a life of crime under the raider. Like father like son.

He knows I know, Jan. So, if I don't make it to the day he's captured, promise me to stay strong. I shall always love you.

Would it have led to Roman's arrest if Janice had received it? He murdered Ted before he had a chance to send the letter. Faith needed to know her dad's true identity before she became his next victim. Since I was now the only living person who knew about the letter, it was up to me to bring Faith's granddad justice. I feared the letter alone would not be enough evidence in court, releasing him with the knowledge that Faith and I were aware of what he did. I needed to find the documents Ted had discovered. They must have followed him to Ted's house. I needed to get into that house. My mind wandered back to one of Ted's letters, which I had barely skimmed over since I didn't think it necessary.

I returned to the pile of letters, picking a tiny stack from the top to begin reading. On the day he locked himself out of his home, he hid a backup key. But what happened to the extra key?

My haste resulted in clumsiness, and I knocked the rest of the letters off the bed. As the pages dropped to the floor, they mixed together, making them indistinguishable. But I was adamant about not giving up. I gathered them all into one pile and then separated the ones Ted wrote more recently from the ones he wrote in his younger years. My head rose with elation as I found it within a few minutes after starting the two piles. My gaze followed the sentence about the hidden spare key.

"...The next time I forget my key, I won't be stuck with wet rain-soaked bread. I hid the spare key beneath the hydrangea, and I hope I remember I put it there."

My optimism dwindled as I searched my imagination for a visual image of a hydrangea.

"You've barely touched your dinner, sweetie." Louise reappeared at the door. My eyes shifted towards my alarm clock, then to my window. The night sky gleamed in; time had passed so quickly. I had expected to get to the house while it was still light, but I felt no less determined now it was dark. I thought Louise could be of some help.

"What's a hydrangea?"

She uttered a chuckle as she looked back at me with interest, "a type of flower, why?"

"It's just something I need for the school project."

It wasn't a lie. It *was* something that I needed for the school project. Only, I hadn't revealed the truth about the topic idea to Louise. Once she first learnt of the murder of Ted White, she was preparing to move all of us out of Dawnton. That was until she realised her finances wouldn't allow her to move closer to the city. Moving entirely away from the area would mean leaving behind the memories she had with the twin's dad; to her, it would be like losing him again. She claimed that removing me from private education during my last year would upset my grades. Still, I knew she was only trying to persuade herself. I knew Louise felt frightened and remorseful for us all still staying at Dawnton, so I decided it was best not to tell her.

"When you were younger, we had a few bushes of them in the garden."

Pink petals brushed against my cheeks as I toppled onto the freshly mowed grass. Louise lifted me by my arms and removed the grass fragments glued to my lips.

"Woopsie daisy baby!" She sang it in tune. Then she placed me on her lap, brushing the grass off my dungarees.

"Mummy will be picking you up soon."

My mouth trembled. Mummy and dread became strongly intertwined.

"I know, sweetie, I'm going to get you out of there, I promise."

I placed my head on her chest as she combed her soft fingers through my hair.

"What the pink ones?"

Louise's smile was contagious.

"Milo damaged the little garden I had, so now I leave it just as a lawn."

She turned her gaze to my window, "There be plenty of photos of hydrangeas on the internet, however."

She continued to pick up the tray, which still had a full plate of food on it.

"Do you want me to cook you something instead of this?"

I didn't want her to think I thought it tasted bad.

"No, it's okay. I ate so much in school today."

She proceeded back down the steps with my tray, smiling her delighted grin.

I no longer had to rely on my imagination to create a picture of a hydrangea. It was now so vivid in my mind. I grabbed the letter and dashed out of the house, making no noise as I passed Louise in the kitchen.

I had no backup plan in case someone stole the key. I wouldn't let the thoughts get that far in my head. It had to be precisely where he had written it to be.

The trees that lined the path leading up to the house were towering, with tree trunks that suggested their old age. It reminded me of another of Ted's letters, where he emphasised his disapproval of the chopping of the trees. His well-coordinated protest seemed to have worked, I thought. An automatic light switched on as I approached the front door, which flickered the longer I stayed there. I didn't pay attention to the outdoor plants during my first two visits to Faith's house. So seeing the skeletal sticks sitting in the soil sparked a crisis. There was nothing to tell one plant from another, much less know if it was a hydrangea. Flowers bloomed at such an inconvenient time of year.

I re-read the sentences in the letter to see if anything was further said about where it was. For all I knew, Faith's dad could have buried the key at the side of the house. After the unsuccessful read, I switched on my phone's torch, hoping it would catch the shine of the key. I began walking from one side of the soil to the other while hunched over, repeating my steps again. My back began to ache after a time, so using one hand for support, I straightened my posture to stand upright. I had a fleeting hope that they had forgotten to lock the front door. My hand grabbed the door handle but another bare yet potted plant by the welcome mat drew my attention. Was it possible that this was the hydrangea? I dragged the plant pot closer to me, hearing concrete scraping with the length I pulled it. Whatever was under the pot was being dragged along with it. I lifted my foot and knocked the pot over with my whole body's strength. Mounds of soil poured out on the welcome mat and a gleaming silver key greeted me.

It only took one step over the fallen plant pot to reach the key in the door. My heart leapt with terror as the door clicked shut behind me. I traced my hand along the wall, searching for the light switch until I felt it raise under my hand. Boxes still cluttered the kitchen. I tiptoed through in an attempt to silence my footsteps. Because despite how it appeared, I wasn't entirely convinced the house was empty.

Surprisingly, most of the house appeared to be open plan. I focused on the rooms separated from the open design. I made my way over to each room but not a single door opened to anything that resembled an office. A door with double locks stood further along the length of the house. I assumed it to be the garden door, and the locks were to prevent a break-in. But I had already seen the garden through the French doors at the back of the house. This meant that rather than stopping people from entering, they installed the locks to conceal what was behind the door.

My entire focus was on the locks. I got closer, knowing I had little chance of finding the key to open them. But at a closer look, the locks didn't seem as sturdy. Did Faith's dad use them as a temporary hold for stronger ones to replace them? They were the type of locks Louise put on the twins' baby gates when they were younger. Macy and Maddie used to rock themselves on the gates to get the lock to lift. Perhaps I could do the same. I pushed the handle down and began to pull the door back and forth to gauge the strength of the locks. I slammed my body against it, feeling the nails that held the bracket to the door pull out and clink on the floor.

Another automatic light switch. Brown panelling from the house continued into the room. Empty mahogany bookcases filled three walls, while the fourth wall remained bare. In the centre, a grey-green button-tufted chair sat with a walnut desk. Several cream filing cabinets sat behind the chair, strikingly out of sync with the rest of the room's age. It had to be his office. Without hesitation, I dashed to the filing cabinets and opened each drawer from top to bottom. Papers upon papers of nothing. The first cabinet was filled with water and gas bills, tax information, and appointment letters. But I knew documents identifying him as Roman Woodson wouldn't be so easy to find. I scoured the room for any possible hiding spots. Anything out of place would be noticeable because of the room's sparse decor. An originally unnoticed draw on the desk came to my attention. I sat on the chair, causing a cloud of dust to rise and pulled on the draw handle. I underestimated the strength needed to open it, as it appeared something had jammed it shut. I stood up and yanked at the draw with equal weight on both legs. The handle flung off, propelling me back in the seat.

For a while, my thoughts were silent. I wasn't sure if the fight to open the draw was even worth it. I put my hands in the pocket of my school blazer and felt the chill of the key on my fingertips. My mind sparked with an idea. I removed the key from my pocket and inserted it into the gap between the drawer's top and the desk. I slid the key back and forth along the drawer's edge, then pushed it further. The pressure eased. I tilted the key down and pulled the drawer out towards me. A brown envelope sat alone. I turned the envelope over and pulled the paper out. My heart accelerated as the name looked back at me. Roman Woodson.

"Hello, Melissa."

A voice thrust my body back. My gut plummeted as my gaze lifted. I used the last of my mental strength to keep the room from spinning. Faith's dad stood before me.

Chapter Fifteen
Faith

Seeing the name dried the words from our mouths. Jasmine gazed at me as if I had a response. I had none. We watched as two branches grew from his name.

"His parents?" Jasmine questioned.

From the branches, two names sprouted. Matilda Woodson and Roman Woodson Sr.

Haze obstructed my vision; all my limbs became paralysed as I collapsed to the ground. An agonising pain wounded my chest. I tried to gaze down by tilting my head, but all I could do was move my eyes. Blood soaked my school shirt.

My eyes opened to Jasmine's ringtone. We were still both staring at the ever-growing list of names on the computer screen. I peered down at my seated body; my limbs moved okay. She reached into the back pocket of her tight skinny jeans and yanked her phone out. Her phone screen displayed Mum's name. I kept a close eye on Jasmine's lips as she began to reply to Mum. Concerned, she bit her bottom lip. I straightened my slouched body.

"What's happened?" I faintly questioned.

Jasmine let out a gasp, "there was a break-in at your house!"

Not long after the phone call, Mum and Dad came bursting back into the hotel room.

"Right, now, let's get to the car," Mum said and led me by the arm out of the room once I put on my coat and shoes. She brought me to the car as Dad checked out of the hotel. Mum's foot tapped with impatience as we waited at the car door.

"What's taking him so long?"

Dad's real name was all that overtook my brain. No records under his name indicated he was even an orphan. So why would he choose to lie about such a thing? When I was near him, my whole body tightened. He wasn't the man he presented himself to be. I glanced across at Mum; her breathing was shallow.

"The police should have got to the house by now."

I figured mentioning the police would reassure her.

"No, your father thought it would be best if they were not called."

After a while, Dad arrived and unlocked the car doors to let us in. I chose to remain silent. Throughout the trip home, I caught him glancing through the rear-view mirror. The look in his eyes made me feel uneasy. I mentally prepared responses in case he asked why I was so quiet, but he didn't speak a word to me.

The inside light glared through the front window of the house.

"Do you think they're still in there?" Mum whispered, her hand covering her mouth.

Dad got out of the car and shut the door, ignoring her question. Mum returned my stare. As I glanced through the car window, I saw Dad walking calmly with the front door key in his hand.

"So, there wasn't a break-in?" I asked as I returned my gaze to Mum.

117

"Yes, there was. The security cameras captured it. Your father saw it; I had no idea we had any cameras in the house. Luckily, your father is so forward-thinking."

I pulled on the handle beside me to open the car door. Dad's office was the only area he put cameras. The day he installed them, he was adamant Mum wouldn't allow cameras anywhere else. He knew who was inside, or else he wouldn't have felt so comfortable walking in alone. He would have called the police to do it for him.

"No!" Mum's voice was stern and I'd never heard her speak with such authority before. But the house was beckoning me inside. I dashed into the house, leaving the car door wide open. Adrenaline fuelled my bones as I sprinted through to the opposite end of the house. Scattered nails were in the open doorway of the office. From inside, a faint voice spoke in stuttering phrases. The voice was hauntingly familiar. Melissa?

Melissa stood frozen in front of Dad; her hands clutched something behind her back. As she looked at me, terror shone in her eyes. Her chest began to expand in response to her deeper breathing. She brushed past me and started running out of the house.

"I'll see if she makes it home safely; after all, it's dark outside." It was the first thing Dad had spoken to me all evening, and his voice lacked genuine worry.

Then something jolted my head forward. I looked back onto the empty street, breathless. I was on the run. The ground reflected the night sky. My heart pounded with fear. I was clasping something in my hands. Papers. The documents of Roman Woodson.

My head jerked back, and I stood alone in dad's office. My hair stood on end as the stillness began to creep around me. I walked out, putting my heel first on each step. The wall steadied my balance, and I watched my hand tremble. Where was Dad?

My head jolted forward again. I was losing stamina. My eyes peered around the shadowing streets for a place to catch my breath. An entry to an alleyway. There should be no danger to me there. I hobbled over with panting breath to the inside wall; the lamppost projected light on either side of me. My breathing was starting to settle, so I tucked the papers into the pocket of my school blazer. I moved my hand around my pocket instinctively, feeling the ridges of a key and then the elastic of a hair tie. I collected my hair into one hand before hearing the elastic snap. Brown hair flowed to the front of my eyes. Melissa's hair. This was Melissa's vision.

I inwardly gasped. Mum was still out in the car. My pace quickened until I took a step outside the front door. Mum hunched over, massaging the tops of her arms for comfort. Her hot cheeks glistened with tears as they rolled down her face. As I moved nearer, I realised her cheeks weren't reddened from tears; they were bruises. She said nothing. There was no sign of the car in the deserted front drive. Dad must have taken it to get Melissa. I had to arrive before him. My gaze returned to Mum.

"I'll be back for you, I promise."

My heart broke at her response, but I couldn't abandon Melissa. The route appeared in my memory as if I had been there before. She was in an alleyway, a location that a car couldn't easily get to, so I knew it brought me some time.

Despite my exhaustion, my legs extended to leaps. The cold air prickled my cheeks as I made a sharp turn down a narrow road. The winds force propelled me ahead. As I approached an empty parking lot, my pulse became louder. My eyes darted in all directions before settling on an alleyway that would lead me out. A car's exhaust turned my attention away. An all-black, well-kept Mercedes-Benz drove up to the car park. It was Dad's car. I dashed across the alleyway, hoping he didn't see me as he parked his car in one of the open spaces. But as I began to sprint, our eyes locked and time seemed to slow. Visions overwhelmed my mind. Family images flashed through my head and it was unmistakable that I had never appeared in one of them. Before my coma, it was as if I had never existed to any of them. As though I didn't exist at all. I had no connection to anybody in my family except Ted White. My memory returned me to the hotel, reading the result on the computer screen. There was a reason why I was here. And I had finally uncovered it.

Dad's brown eyes glowed with spikes that pierced my pupils. Time was no longer slowed. I continued sprinting as fast as my legs could carry me until I reached the alleyway entrance. It matched exactly what I had been seeing. The lamppost stood at the end, marking the start of a tangle of streets leading back to my house.

"Faith?" Melissa crouched on the floor; her face contoured in horror as she looked up at me. I turned back to look for Dad. He abandoned his car. I watched him move closer, a malicious grin printed on his face and a brown shotgun resting against his forearm. I backed further into the alleyway, protecting Melissa with my arm. Her whimpers had become audible and I was doing everything I could to avoid doing the same. The nearer Dad got, the slower his torturous footsteps became. He pulled himself around the alleyway wall and positioned himself parallel to us. The light bouncing from the lamppost lit up the top of his shotgun like a flashlight. He raised the gun and cocked it. His sight set on Melissa.

"If you shoot, they'll know you did it." My voice quivered as I spoke. I needed to divert Roman's focus away from the trigger. His eyes turned to me.

"I've told the police of our location." My teeth chattered as I swallowed the lie. Roman moved the gun to point at me, "but I didn't specify it was you."

I spoke within a breath, and I immediately followed it up, "a double murder means the rest of your life in prison, and everything you've worked for, gone."

My words were working to keep him from firing the gun. He wore a focused expression. There was a backlog of crimes he had committed, so I hoped the thought of the police catching him would make him rethink.

"Or, you can leave now, and we promise to say nothing."

He pointed his gun back at Melissa. I increased my voice to be more forceful; tears made him become a silhouette, "save her, and we won't say a word to anyone. We are the only ones who know who you are."

He began to approach closer. The gun's tip reached us before he did. He drew his gun and pointed it at Melissa's chest.

Chapter Sixteen
Melissa

I tightly closed my eyes. My heart pounded against the tip of the gun. I looked out the car window; the grass was blurry with the road. A big yellow-haired lady sat next to me; I felt scared, but not of her. She pulled me away from Mummy. Mummy would hurt me. My belly used to rumble, but Mummy said she could never hear it. The men that came to the house were so scary. They used to talk to me with words I didn't understand, but the words made my belly turn upside-down. The big yellow-haired lady was bringing me away. She told me we were going to live with Aunty Louise. Aunty Louise kept my belly full. She never shouted when I cried. She read me stories and held me tight when there was a scary part; then, she rocked me back and forward until I fell asleep. Aunty Louise kept me safe. She kept Michael safe too. My brother was bigger than me, but he wasn't strong enough to stop the nasty men from coming near me. She hugged me so tight and gave me her promise, "you don't have to feel scared; I've got you now forever, my sweet."

The gun's grip on my chest abruptly vanished. I blinked open my eyes. Faith had pushed the end of the gun down, causing the imbalanced weight to topple over his shoulder. The gun lay between us. It was now in closer reach to Faith than Roman. But she wouldn't be able to fight his strength of him alone. In the same split second, I joined Faith in raising the shotgun to our eye level. Our hands quivered with exhaustion as we pointed it towards Roman. Faith's finger was hovering over the trigger. He raised his hands and began backing away. A loud blast ruptured my eardrums. The force threw us backwards, slamming our bodies onto the concrete. Despite the excruciating pain that had crushed my bones, I pushed myself from the ground. She was on target. A pool of blood began to spread around Roman's head. I arched my neck to see Faith, but she was already kneeling beside me. Her skin glowed soft yellow and her face was bright with joy. She seemed to be in no pain at all.

"Are you hurt?" My voice was barely audible. Faith took my grazed hand in hers and placed it on her lap.

"You can continue to live," she said, her smile remaining intact on her face. I thought of invisible injuries that would force her to accept death.

"You can too, right?" I answered in a worried tone.

Her eyes welled up with tears. I pulled my hand from her lap and felt a sting as I slid it into my blazer pocket in search of my phone. I needed to call for an ambulance to save her.

"No, Mel. We achieved what was set out to do; my time here is up."

I pulled my hand back out of my pocket. "What are you talking about?"

Her voice was calm, "you can return back to your side of the earth.

As I snorted a chuckle, my chest throbbed, "well, what side is this?"

Was this all a game to her? It had done the opposite if she had hoped it would brighten my mood. She inhaled, "it's the world parallel to it."

Her tone matched her serious expression. Something in my gut told me this wasn't a lie.

"The time on the other side has paused," she continued. "It was not your destiny to die; everyone gets a second chance. A parallel world buds, and you can re-live the moments until your passing."

Doubt began to rise.

"Who are you?" I questioned; the sternness clipped my words.

"There are two parts to your consciousness." She remained calm as she gazed into my eyes, "I'm you."

I had an unspoken bond with her. She never failed to show up when I needed her most. She pulled through and saved me in every situation. As the pieces of my brain began to fit together, I refused to believe them.

"No! You're Faith Mathews. You have a Mum called Janice; you moved to Dawnton to live in your dead granddad's house. That is all!"

I attempted to straighten my back to sit up through my discomfort, but my weakened muscles pushed me back to the floor.

"I was assigned to their family to find you. I never existed to them on the other side." She blinked a tear, "we achieved what was set out to do, Mel."

My thoughts twisted, "and what would have happened if we didn't?"

She stood up from her knelt position, her smile no longer bright as it had been. She lifted my arms and cupped her hands under my armpits to make me stand. I grunted in pain.

"What happens to you now?" I asked, struggling to maintain my balance even with her support.

Her body began to fade to slight transparency.

"Faith?"

She stayed silent. Like a ghost could, she stepped through me. I whirled around to look behind me; she had vanished. Then my eyes became heavy, and my vision eventually darkened.

***

Breaking news, the infamous Murderer, Shotgun, was shot dead in the early morning hours in a parking lot alleyway in Dawnton town. Roman Woodson, 45, was identified as the perpetrator. As he fired his gun, the bullet rebounded and hit his own head, giving the 16-year-old victim, Melissa, a lucky escape. Her statement reads, 'I'm so fortunate to be alive right now.' And when asked what has kept her going after such a traumatic event, her response was simply; I guess faith pulled me through.

About the Author

Angel Bloxham began writing "He Knows I Know," her most recent work, when she was seventeen years old and unsure of what to do after losing her phone. She decided to pick up a book to read at the same time. That just so happened to be a murder mystery. Since then, she has become addicted to reading the genre; in fact, it's why she chose it to be the genre of her first published book.

Ingram Content Group UK Ltd.
Milton Keynes UK
UKHW010632220523
422140UK00001B/6